Two magnolias-and-mistletoe-inspired holiday stories from the bestselling author of more than thirty romantic, humorous novels.

Laughter and love combine in Sandra Hill's BLUE CHRISTMAS—with a touch of Elvis magic. Wealthy Wall Street businessman Clayton Jessup III has only one reason for arriving in Memphis a few days before Christmas—to sell off his inheritance, an embarrassingly kitschy hotel named The Blue Suede Suites. His feelings for the Land of Elvis are dark: his long-dead Memphis mother abandoned him and his dad when Clay was a baby, and now Clay wants nothing to do with a southern legacy that couldn't be more different from his sophisticated big-city life.

But then he steps in trouble—literally—when he confronts the bizarre group of Elvis impersonators who've set up a living Nativity scene on his property. One slip of a wingtip in some sheep poop lands Clay in the care of gorgeous Annie Fallon, whose big-haired Elvis-girlfriend get-up can't hide her wholesome, sexy appeal. Annie and her brothers have set up the Nativity scene to earn some badly needed money for their struggling dairy farm.

The last thing she needs is an angry Yankee with a concussion and a come-hither smile . . .

In JINX CHRISTMAS, sexy NASCAR star Lance Caslow makes a last-ditch effort to win back his ex-wife Brenda. Five years ago, his reckless pursuit of racetrack fame tore them apart and broke Brenda's heart. Now Lance shows up in Louisiana determined to make things right this Christmas, not just for himself and Brenda, but for their young daughter, Patti.

He's got his work cut out for him, and desperate measures are needed. Lance will do *anything* to prove he's worthy of Brenda's trust again—even join the Cajun Christmas show starring a raucous Cajun family whose menfolk dance for charity events in little more than a smile . . .

D1548493

A Dixie Christmas

by

Sandra Hill

Bell Bridge Books

This is a work of fiction. Names, characters, places and incidents are either the products of the author's imagination or are used fictitiously. Any resemblance to actual persons (living or dead,) events or locations is entirely coincidental.

Bell Bridge Books
PO BOX 300921
Memphis, TN 38130
ISBN: 978-1-61194-080-0
eISBN: 978-1-61194-073-2

Bell Bridge Books is an Imprint of BelleBooks, Inc.

Printed and bound in the United States of America.

All rights reserved. No part of this book may be reproduced in any form or by any electronic or mechanical means, including information storage and retrieval systems, without permission in writing from the publisher, except by a reviewer, who may quote brief passages in a review.

Blue Christmas copyright 1998 by Sandra Hill
Originally published as "Fever" in the *Blue Christmas* anthology
Jinx Christmas copyright 1999 by Sandra Hill

We at BelleBooks enjoy hearing from readers.
Visit our websites – www.BelleBooks.com and www.BellBridgeBooks.com.

10 9 8 7 6 5 4 3 2 1

Cover design: Debra Dixon
Interior design: Hank Smith
Photo credits:
Legs and Background - © Madartists | Dreamstime.com

:Ldac:01:

Reader Letter

Dear Readers:

A wise editor once told me that in the best of all books the reader should both laugh and cry. That's what I wish for you with JINX CHRISTMAS and BLUE CHRISTMAS, a lot of smiles and perhaps a tear here and there. The holiday season is made for poignancy and humor.

BLUE CHRISTMAS, a stand-alone story, was originally published in 1998 as "Fever" in the long out-of-print anthology, BLUE CHRISTMAS. It has been tweaked and updated, as has the short novella JINX CHRISTMAS, which has never been published, but was available for a short time on my website. JINX CHRISTMAS can stand alone, as well, although it is linked loosely with my Cajun/Jinx series. See my website for more details.

I also hope you'll check out my anthology 'TWAS THE NIGHT, which is available in print, ebook, and unabridged audiobook at Audible.com, Amazon.com and iTunes. The book was written Round-Robin style with Trish Jensen and Kate Holmes (aka Anne Avery), so that it reads more like a novel than an anthology. It is a tweaked and updated version of our laugh-out-loud funny HERE COMES SANTA CLAUS.

Authors often cringe at having to go back and reread their old books, but I must say with a shameless lack of humility that these books are really good. And they can be read over and over each holiday season.

Let me know what you think of this anthology. I welcome reader letters. And come visit my website (www.sandrahill.net) and my Facebook page (Sandra Hill Author) for details on past and coming books, videos, genealogy charts and other good stuff.

Wishing you the happiest Christmas ever, and, as always, wishing you smiles in your reading,

—*Sandra Hill*

Dedication

This anthology is dedicated to my four sons and three grandchildren who love my love of the Christmas season. I'm not saying I over-decorate, but I do put up a Christmas tree the day after Thanksgiving and I do wax with nostalgia over each and every special ornament uncovered, including all the handmade mice that Grandma Campbell made. I need at least four weeks to savor the anticipation of this blessed day.

But especially this book is dedicated to my son Rob who once asked me when he was a little boy: "Are God and Santa Claus related?"

Doesn't that say it all?

Chapter One

They should have named it "Heartbreak Hotel."

"Oh, my gawd! It's George Strait."

"Where? Where? Oooh, oooh, oooh! I swear, Mabel, I'm so excited I'm gonna pee my pants."

Clayton Jessup, III was about to enter his suite at the Blue Suede Suites when he heard the high-pitched squeals of the two blue-haired ladies in matching neon pink, "Elvis Lives" sweat shirts.

He glanced over his shoulder to see who was generating so much excitement and saw no one. *Uh-oh!* In an instant, he realized that they thought he was the George person . . . probably some Memphis celebrity. Even worse, they were pep-stepping briskly toward him with huge smiles plastered across their expectant faces, and autograph books drawn to the ready.

"Open the damn door," he snarled at the wizened old bellhop, whose kidney-spotted hands were fumbling with the key.

"I'm tryin', I'm tryin'. You don't wanna get caught by any of these country music fanatics. Last week over on Beale Street, they tore off every bit of a construction worker's clothes for souvenirs, right down to his skivvies, just 'cause they thought he was Kenny Chesney."

"Who the hell is Kenny Chesney?"

"You're kidding, right?" the bellhop said, casting him a sideways once-over of disbelief.

Clay grabbed the key out of the bellhop's hand and inserted it himself. Just before the women were ready to pounce, gushing, "Oooh, George. Yoo hoo!", the door swung open and they escaped. Leaning against the closed door, he exhaled with a loud whoosh of relief.

He heard one of the women say, "Mabel, I don't think that was George. He wasn't wearing a cowboy hat, and George never goes anywhere without his trademark cowboy hat."

"Maybe you're right, Mildred," Mabel said.

"Besides, he was too skinny to be George. He looked more like that Richard Gere. A younger version of Richard, I mean."

Richard Gere? Me? Mildred needs a new set of bifocals.

"Richard Gere," Mabel swooned. "Hmmm. Is it possible . . . ? Nah. That guy was taller and leaner than Richard Gere. Besides, Richard Gere is more likely to be off in Tibet with the Dolly Lay-ma, not in Memphis."

"At least we saw Elvis's ghost at Graceland today."

Their voices were fading now; so Clay knew they were walking away.

Dropping his briefcase to the floor, he opened his closed eyes . . . and almost had a heart attack. "Holy shit! What is this?" he asked the bellhop.

"The Roustabout Suite," the bellhop said proudly, shifting from foot to foot with excitement. The dingbat looked absolutely ridiculous in his old-fashioned, red, bellhop outfit, complete with a pillbox hat. "It's the best one in The Blue Suede Suites, next to the Viva Las Vegas and the Blue Hawaii suites, of course. Families with children love it."

"I do not have children," Clay gritted out.

"Aaahh, that's too bad. Some folks think the spirit of Elvis lives in this hotel. Seen 'em myself a time or two. Maybe if you pray to the Elvis spirit, he'll intercede with the Good Lord to rev up your sperm count. Or if the problem is with the little lady, you could . . . uh, why is your face turnin' purple?"

"I do not have children. I am not married. Mind your own damn business."

"Oops!" the bellhop said, ducking his head sheepishly. "Sometimes I talk a mite too much, but I'm a firm believer in Southern hospitality. Yep. Better to be friendly and take a chance than . . . " The fool blathered on endlessly without a care for whether Clay was listening or not. Really, he should be home in a rocking chair, instead of parading around a hotel like an organ grinder's monkey. Another "to do" item to add to his itinerary: check hotel's retirement policy.

Clay turned his back on the rambling old man . . . and groaned inwardly as he recognized that his view from this angle wasn't any better. *The Roustabout Suite. Hell!*

The split-level suite had a miniature merry-go-round in the sitting room. As the carousel horses circled, a pipe organ blasted out carnival music. A candy cotton machine was set up in one corner, and the blasted thing actually worked, if the sickly sweet odor was any indication. Candy apples lay on the bar counter beside a slurpee dispenser in the small kitchenette. The walls were papered with movie posters from the Elvis movie "Roustabout," and the bed was an enlarged version of a tunnel-of-love car. On the bedside table sat a clown lamp and a clock in the form of a Ferris wheel. Up and down went the clown's blinking eyes. Round and round went the clock's illuminated dial. Mixed in with this eclectic collection were quality pieces of furniture, no doubt from the original hotel furnishings.

If Clay didn't have a headache already, this room would surely give him the mother of all migraines. "You can't seriously think I'd stay in this . . . this three-ring circus."

"Well, it was the best we could do on such short notice," the bellhop said, clearly affronted.

"Hee-haw! Hee-haw! Baaaa! Baaaa! Hee-haw!"

For a moment, Clay lowered his head, not sure he wanted to know what those sounds were, coming from outside. Walking briskly across the room, he glanced out the second-floor window . . . then did an amazed double take.

"Oh! Aren't they cute?" the bellhop commented behind him.

"Humph!" Clay grumbled in disagreement. Pulling his electronic pocket organizer from his suit pocket, he clicked to the Memphis directory where he typed in his observations, punctuated with several more "Humph's." It was a word that seemed to slip out of his mouth a lot lately . . . a word his father had used all the time. *Am I turning into a negative, stuffy version of my father now? Is that what I've come to?*

"Hee-haw! Hee-haw! Baaaa! Baaaa! Hee-haw!"

"Oh, Good Lord!" The headache that had been building all day finally exploded behind his eyes—a headache the size of the bizarre "inheritance" he'd come to Tennessee to investigate. Raking his fingers through his close-clipped hair, he gazed incredulously at the scene unfolding on the vacant lot below . . . a property he now happened to own, along with this corny hotel. Neither was his idea of good fortune.

"Hee-haw! Hee-haw! Baaaa! Baaaa! Hee-haw!"

"What the hell is going on?" he asked the bellhop who was now standing in the walk-in closet hanging Clay's garment bag.

"A live Nativity scene."

"Humph!" Clay arched a brow skeptically. It didn't resemble any Nativity scene he'd ever witnessed.

"Did you say humbug?" the bellhop inquired.

"No, I didn't say humbug," he snapped, making a mental note to add an observation in the hotel file of his pocket organizer about the attitude of the staff. *What does the imbecile think I am? A crotchety old man out of a Dickens' novel? Hell, I'm only thirty-three years old. I'm not crotchety. My father was crotchety. I'm not.* "I said *humph*. That's an expression denoting . . . oh, never mind."

He peered outside again. The bellhop was right. Five men, one woman, a baby, a donkey and two sheep were setting up shop in a scene reminiscent of a Monty Python parody, or a bad Saturday Night Live skit. The only thing missing was a camel or two.

Please, God. No camels, Clay prayed quickly, just in case. He wasn't sure how many more shocks he could take today.

The trip this morning from his home in Princeton had been uneventful. He'd managed to clear a backlog of paperwork while his driver transported him in the smooth-riding, oversized Mercedes sedan to Newark Airport. He'd been thinking about ditching the gas guzzler ever since his father died six months ago, but now he had second thoughts. The first-class airline accommodations had been quiet, too, and conducive to work.

The nightmare had begun once he entered the Memphis International Airport terminal. Every refined, well-bred cell in his body had been assaulted by raucous sounds of tasteless music and by the even more tasteless souvenirs of every conceivable Elvis item in the world . . . everything from "Barbie Loves Elvis" dolls to "authentic" plastic mini-flasks of Elvis sweat.

The worst was to come, however.

When Clay had arrived at the hotel to investigate the last of his sizeable inheritance, consisting mostly of blue chip stocks and bonds, he found The Blue Suede Suites. How could his father . . . a conservative Wall Street investment banker, long-time supporter of the symphony, connoisseur of Old Master paintings . . . have bought a hotel named The Blue Suede Suites? And why, for God's sake? More important, why had he kept it a secret since its purchase thirty-five years ago?

But that was beside the point now. His most immediate problem was the yahoos setting up camp outside. He hesitated to ask the impertinent bellhop another question, which was ridiculous. He was in essence his employee. "Who are they?"

The bellhop ambled over next to him. "The Fallons."

"Are they entertainers?"

The bellhop laughed. "Nah. They're dairy farmers."

Dairy farmers? Don't ask. You'll get another stupid non-answer. "Well, they're trespassing on my property. Tell the management when you go down to the lobby to evict them immediately."

"Now, now, sir, don't be actin' hastily. They're just poor orphans tryin' to make a living, and—"

4

"Orphans? They're a little old to be orphans," he scoffed.

"—and besides, it was my idea."

"Your idea?" Clay snorted. Really, he felt as if he'd fallen down some garden hole and landed on another planet.

"Yep. Last week, Annie Fallon was sittin' in the Hound Dog Cafe downstairs, havin' a cup of coffee, lookin' fer all the world like she lost her best friend. She just came from the monthly Holstein Association meeting across the street. You know what Holsteins are, dontcha?"

"Of course, I do," he said with a sniff. *They're cows, aren't they?*

"Turns out Annie and her five brothers are in dire financial straits," the bellhop rambled on, "and it occurred to me, and I tol' her so, too, that with five brothers and a new baby . . . her brother Chet's girlfriend *dropped* their sweet little boy in his lap, so to speak . . . well, they had just enough folks fer a Nativity scene, it bein' Christmas and all. I can't figure how the idea came to me. Like a miracle it was . . . an idea straight out of heaven, if ya ask me." The old man took a deep, wheezy breath, then concluded, "You wouldn't begrudge them a little enterprise like this, wouldja, especially at Christmastime?"

Clay didn't believe in Christmas, never had, but that was none of this yokel's business. "I don't care if it's the Fourth of July. Those . . . those squatters better be gone by the time I get down there, or someone is going to pay. Look at them," he said, sputtering with outrage. "Bad enough they're planting themselves on private land, but they have the nerve to act as if they own the damn place." Hauling wooden frames off a pick-up truck, they were now erecting a three-sided shed, then strewing about the ground hay from two bales.

That wasn't the worst part, though. All of the characters were made up as Elvis versions—*What else!*—of the Nativity figures, complete with fluffed-up hair and sideburns.

The Three Wise Men were tall, lean men in their late teens or early twenties wearing long satin robes of jewel tone colors, covered by short shoulder capes with high stand-up collars. Their garish attire was adorned with enough sequins and glitter to do the tackiest Vegas sideshow proud. They moved efficiently about their jobs in well-worn leather cowboy boots, except for the shepherd in duct-taped sneakers. Belts with huge buckles, like rodeo cowboys usually wore, tucked in their trim waists.

The shepherd, about thirteen years old, wore a knee-high, one-piece sheepskin affair, also belted with a shiny clasp the size of a hubcap. Even the sleeping baby, placed carefully in a rough manger, had its hair slicked up into an Elvis curl, artfully arranged over its forehead.

Joseph was a glowering man in his mid-twenties, wearing a gem-studded burlap gown, a rope belt with the requisite buckle, and scruffy boots. Since he kept checking the infant every couple of minutes, Clay assumed he must be the father.

"Hee-haw! Hee-haw! Baaaa! Baaaa! Hee-haw!"

Clay's attention was diverted to an animal trailer, parked behind the pickup truck, where one of the Wise Men was leading the braying donkey and two sheep, none of which appeared happy to participate in the blessed event. In fact, the donkey dug in its hooves stubbornly—*Do donkeys have hooves?*—as the obviously cursing Wise Man yanked on the lead rope. The donkey got the last word by marking the site with a spray of urine, barely missing the boot of the Wise Man who danced away at the last moment. The sheep deposited their own Nativity "gifts."

Clay would have laughed if he weren't so angry.

Then he noticed the woman.

Lordy, did he notice the woman!

A peculiar heat swept over him then, burning his face, raising hairs on the back of his neck and forearms, even along his thighs and calves, lodging smack dab in his gut, and lower. How odd! It must be anger, he concluded, because he sure as hell wasn't attracted to the woman. Not by a Wall Street longshot!

She was tall—at least five-foot-nine—and skinny as a rail. He could see that, even under her plain blue, ankle-length gown . . . well, as plain as it could be with its overabundant studding of pearls. In tune with her outrageous ensemble, she sported the biggest hair he'd ever seen outside a fifties movie retrospective. The long brunette strands had been teased and arranged into an enormous bowl shape that flipped up on the ends—probably in imitation of Elvis's wife. *What was her name? Patricia? Phyllis? No. Priscilla, that was it.* She must have depleted the entire ozone layer over Tennessee to hold that monstrosity in place. Even from this distance he could see that her eyelids were covered with a tawdry plastering of blue eye shadow and weighted down with false eyelashes. Madonna, she was not . . . neither the heavenly one, nor the rock star with the cone-shaped bra from a few years back.

Still, a strange heat pulsed through his body as he gazed at her.

Does she realize how ridiculous she looks?
Does she care?
Do I care?
Damn straight I do! he answered himself as the woman, leader of the

motley Biblical crew, waved her hands dictatorially, wagged her forefinger and steered the others into their places. Within minutes, they posed statue-like in a Memphis version of the Nativity scene. The only one unfrozen was the shepherd whose clear adolescent voice rang out clearly with "Oh, Holy Night."

Already tourists passing by were pausing, oohing and aahing, and dropping coins and paper money into the iron kettle set in the front. It was only noon, but it was clear to Clay that by the end of the day this group was going to make a bundle.

"Not on my property!" Clay vowed, grabbing his overcoat and making for the door. At the last minute, he paused and handed the clearly disapproving bellhop a five dollar bill.

For some reason, the scowling man made him feel like . . . well, Scrooge . . . and he hadn't even said "Humph!" again. It was absurd to feel guilty. He was a businessman . . . an investment banker specializing in venture capital. He had every right to make a business decision.

"Thank you for your service," he said coolly. "I'm sure I'll be seeing you again during my stay here in Memphis." Clay intended to remain only long enough to complete arrangements for the razing of the hotel and erection of a strip mall on this site and the adjoining property. He expected to complete his work here before the holidays and catch the Christmas Eve shuttle back to New Jersey on Thursday. Not that he had any particular plans that demanded a swift return to Princeton. On the contrary, there was no one waiting for him in the big empty mansion, except for Doris and George Benson, the longtime cook/housekeeper and gardener/driver. No Christmas parties he would mind missing. No personal relationships that would suffer in his absence.

Clay blinked with surprise at his out-of-character, maudlin musings. This hokey Elvis mania that pervaded Memphis must be invading his brain, like a virus. *The Elvis virus. Ha, ha, ha!*

The bellhop's eyes bored into him, and then softened, as if seeing his thoughts.

Clay didn't like the uncomfortable feeling he got under the bellhop's intense stare.

"You really plannin' on kicking the Fallons off your property? At Christmastime?" the bellhop inquired in a condemning tone of voice.

"Damn straight."

"Even the iciest heart can be melted."

Now what the hell does that mean? "Yeah, well, it's going to take a monumental fever in my case because I have plans for that property."

This is the craziest conversation in the world. Why am I even talking to this kook?

"Don't be cruel, my boy. You know what they say about the best laid plans?"

"Am I supposed to understand that?" *Shut up, Jessup. Just ignore him.*

"Sometimes God sticks out his big toe and trips us humans. You might just be in for a big stumble."

God? Big toe? The man is nuts. "Lock up on your way out," Clay advised, opening the hallway door. Time to put a stop to this nonsense . . . the bellhop, the hotel, the Nativity scene, the whole freakin' mess.

But damned if the impertinent old fart didn't begin singing some Elvis song about cold, cold hearts as Clay closed the door behind him, thus getting in the last word.

All shook up! . . .

"This is the dumbest damn thing you've ever conned us into, Annie."

"Tsk-tsk," Annie told her brother Chet in stiff-lipped *sotto voce.* "We're supposed to be statues. No talking. Furthermore, St. Joseph should *not* be swearing."

A flush crept up the face of her oldest brother, who was handsome, even with the exaggerated Elvis hairdo. Chet was the kind of guy who would probably make a young girl's heart stop even if he were bald.

Good looks aside, her heart went out to Chet. He was twenty-five, only three years younger than she, and so very solemn for his age. Well, he had good reason, she supposed. He'd certainly never hesitated over taking responsibility for raising his baby, Jason, when his girlfriend Emmy Lou "abandoned" the infant to his care a month ago. Even before that, he'd tried hard to be the man of the family ever since their parents died in a car accident ten years ago, changing overnight from a carefree teenager to a weary adult.

Well, they'd all changed with that tragedy. No dwelling on what couldn't be helped.

"There's no one around now," Chet pointed out defensively.

That was true. It was lunch hour and a Sunday; so, only a few people had straggled by thus far. But tourist sidewalk traffic past their panorama on Blues Street, just off the famous Beale Street, should pick up soon. Yesterday, their first day trying out this enterprise, had brought in an amazing seven hundred dollars in tips between eleven a.m. and five p.m. Annie was hoping that in the five days remaining before Christmas they would be able to earn another three thousand dollars, enough to save the farm, so to speak.

"I feel like an absolute fool," Chet grumbled.

"Me, too," her other four brothers concurred with a unified groan.

"Wayne keeps trying to bite my butt," Johnny added. "I swear he's the meanest donkey in the entire world. Pure, one hundred proof jackass, if you ask me."

"He is *not* mean," Jerry Lee argued. The only one Wayne could abide was Jerry Lee, who'd bred him for a 4-H project five years ago. "Wayne senses that you don't like him, and he's trying to get your attention."

"By biting my butt?"

Everyone laughed at that.

"I had a girl once who bit my butt—" Roy started to say.

Annie gasped. "Roy Fallon! If you say one more word, I swear I'll soap your mouth out when we get home. I don't care if you are twenty-two years old."

Everyone laughed some more. Except for Annie.

"Your sheep keep nuzzling this fleece outfit you made me wear," Johnny continued to gripe. He directed his complaint now at Annie. "I think they think I'm one of their cousins."

Ethel and Lucy were Annie's pets. She'd won them when they were only baby lambs in a grange raffle two years ago.

"Stop your whining, boys," she snapped. "Do you think *I'm* enjoying myself? My scalp itches. My skin is probably breaking out in zits, like a popcorn machine. I'm surely straining some muscles in my eyelids with these false eyelashes. And I'm just praying that the barn roof doesn't cave in before we earn enough money for its repair. Or that the price of milk doesn't drop again. Or that we'll be able to afford this semester at vet school for Roy. And—"

"Don't blame this sideshow on me," Roy chimed in. "It's not my fault the government cut the student aid program."

"Oh, Roy, don't get your sideburns in a dither," she said, already regretting her sharp words.

"Or get your duck's ass hairdo in a backwind," Hank taunted.

Annie shot Hank a scowl, and continued, "No one's to blame, Roy. Our problems have been piling up for a long time."

"Well, I'll tell you one thing. If anyone from school comes by, I'm outta here, barn roof or no barn roof," Jerry Lee asserted. At fifteen, peer approval was critical, and dressing up as an Elvis Wise Man probably didn't cut many points with the cheerleading squad.

"You're just worried that Sally Sue Sorenson will see you," Hank teased.

"Am not," Jerry Lee argued, despite his red face.

"Shhhh," Annie cautioned.

A group of tourists approached, and Annie's family froze into their respective parts. Johnny, her youngest brother—*God bless him*—broke loose with an absolutely angelic version of "Silent Night." He must have inherited his singing talent from their parents, who'd been unsuccessful Grand Ole Opry wannabees. The rest of them could barely carry a tune.

In appreciation, the group, which included a man, a woman and three young children, waited through the entire song, then dropped a five dollar bill into the kettle, while several couples following in their wake dropped a bunch of dollar bills each, along with some change. Thank God for the Christmas spirit.

After they passed by, Roy picked up on their interrupted conversation. "Actually, Jerry Lee, don't be too quick to discount the appeal of this Elvis stuff. Being an Elvis lookalike could be a real chick magnet for some babes."

"You've been hanging around barns too long," Jerry Lee scoffed, but there was a note of uncertainty in his voice. Roy was a first year vet student and graduate of the University of Memphis. Jerry Lee wasn't totally sure his big brother, at twenty-two, hadn't picked up a few bits of male-female wisdom.

"He's bullshittin' you," Hank interjected with a laugh, ignoring the glare Annie flashed his way for the coarse language. Hank was a high school senior, a football player, and the self-proclaimed stud of the family.

Jerry Lee gave Roy a dirty look for his ill-advice. Obviously, Hank ranked as the better "chick" expert.

"What do you think, Annie?" Roy asked, chuckling at Jerry Lee's gullibility.

"How would I know what attracts women? I haven't had a date in two years. Then it was with Frankie Wilks, the milk tank driver."

"And he resembles the back end of a hound dog more than Elvis," Hank remarked with a hoot of laughter at his own joke.

"That was unkind, Hank," Annie chastised, "just because he's a little . . . hairy."

They all made snorting sounds of ridicule.

Frankie Wilks had a bushy beard and mustache and a huge mop of frizzy hair. Masses of hair covered his forearms and even peeked out at the neck of his milk company uniform. Hirsute would be an understatement.

"You could go out with guys if you wanted to," Chet offered softly. "You don't have to give up your life for us or the farm. It was different when we were younger, but—"

"Uh-oh!" Roy said.

Everyone stopped talking and stiffened to attention.

A man was stomping down the sidewalk toward them, having emerged from the hotel entrance. He wore a conservative black business suit, so finely cut it must be custom-made, with a snow white shirt and a dark striped tie, spit-shined wing-tip shoes and a black cashmere overcoat that probably cost as much as a new barn roof.

He was a taller, leaner, younger version of Richard Gere, with the same short-clipped dark hair. He would have been heart-stopping handsome if it weren't for the frown lines that seemed to be etched permanently about his flaming eyes and tight-set mouth. How could a man so young be so disagreeable in appearance?

Despite his demeanor, Annie felt a strange heat rush through her, just gazing at him. It was embarrassment, of course. What woman enjoyed looking like a tart in front of a gorgeous man?

Unfortunately, Annie suspected that the flame in his eyes was directed toward them. And she had a pretty good idea who he was, too. Clayton Jessup, III, the new owner of The Blue Suede Suites and the vacant lot where they had set up their Nativity scene.

The kindly couple that managed the hotel, David and Marion Bloom, had given them permission for the Nativity scene when Annie had asked several days ago. "After all, the lot has been vacant for more than thirty years," Marion had remarked. "It's about time someone made use of it."

But when Annie and Chet had stopped in the hotel a short time ago, where David and Marion had also been nice enough to let them use an anteroom for changing Jason, they soon realized that everyone at the hotel was in an uproar. The new owner had arrived, unannounced, and he intended to raze the site and erect a strip shopping mall. As if Memphis needed another mall! Didn't the man recognize the sentimental value of the hotel and this lot? No, she guessed a man like him wouldn't. Money would be his bottom line.

Just before Mr. Jessup got to them, some tourists paused and listened with "oohs" and "aaahs" of appreciation, dropping more paper money and change into their kettle. The boys stood rock still, but Annie saw the gleam of interest in their eyes at one petite blonde woman in gray wool slacks and a cardigan over a peach colored turtleneck that stood staring at them for a long time. There was a hopeless sag to her shoulders until Hank winked at her, and she burst out with a little laugh.

Drawing the sides of his overcoat back, and planting his hands on slim hips, Mr. Jessup glared at them, his lips curling with disdain on getting a close-up view of their attire. At least he had the courtesy to wait till the tourists passed by before snarling, "What the hell are you doing on my property?"

The baby's eyes shot open, and he began to whimper at the harsh voice.

"We have permission," Chet said, his voice as frosty as Mr. Jessup's while he leaned over and soothed his child. "Hush, now. Back to sleep, son," he crooned, rocking the manger slightly.

Annie tried to explain, "Mr. and Mrs. Bloom told us it would be all right. We'll only be here for a few days, and—"

He put up a hand to halt her words. "You won't be here for even a few more hours." He peered down at his watch . . . probably one of those Rolex things, equal in value to the mortgage on their farm . . . and gritted out, "You have exactly fifteen minutes to vacate these premises, or I'll have the police evict you forcibly. So, Ms. Fallon, stop fluttering those ridiculous eyelashes at me."

He knows our surname. Not a good sign! "I was not fluttering."

"Hey, it's not necessary to yell at our sister," Roy yelled. He, Hank, Jerry Lee and Johnny were coming up behind Annie, to form a protective flank. Chet had taken Jason out of the manger and was holding him to his shoulder, as if Mr. Jessup might do the infant bodily harm.

"Furthermore, those animals better not have done any damage," Mr. Jessup continued and proceeded to walk toward the shed where Wayne was hee-hawing and the sheep were bleating, as if sensing some disaster in progress.

"No! Don't!" they all shouted in warning.

Too late.

Mr. Jessup slipped on a pile of sheep dung. Righting himself, he noticed Wayne's back leg shoot out. To avoid the kick, he spun on his ankle. Annie could almost hear the tendons tearing as his ankle twisted. His expensive shoes, now soiled, went out from under him, and the man went down hard, on his back, with his head hitting a small rock with an ominous crack.

"I'm going to sue your eyelashes off," Mr. Jessup said on a moan, just before he passed out.

Chapter Two

A boy like me, a girl like you . . . uh-oh!

He was drunk . . . as a skunk.

Well, not actually drunk. More like under the influence of pain killers. But the effect was the same. Three sheets to a Memphis wind.

"Oh, I wish I was *not* in the land of Dixie," Mr. Jessup belted out. He'd been singing nonstop for the past five minutes.

Annie and the cute emergency room intern exchanged a look.

Annie tried to get him to lie down on the table. "Mr. Jessup, you really should settle—"

"Call me Clay." He flashed her a lopsided grin, accompanied by the most amazing, utterly adorable dimples. Then he resumed his rendition of Dixie with a stanza ending, " . . . *strange* folks there are not forgotten."

Geez!

"I wish I'd bought that tee shirt I saw at the airport." Mr. Jessup . . . rather, Clay . . . stopped singing for a moment to inject that seemingly irrelevant thought. "Its logo said, `Elvis Is Dead, And I'm Not Feelin' So Good Myself.' Ha, ha, ha!"

"He's having a rather . . . um, strange allergic reaction. Or perhaps I just gave him a little too much medication," the young doctor mumbled, casting a sheepish glance toward the other busy cubicles to see if any of his colleagues had overheard.

"No kidding, Doctor McDreamy!" Annie remarked. Clay was now leading an orchestra in his own version of "Flight of the Bumble Bee." She didn't think Rimsky-Korsakov had actual bzzz-ing sounds in his original opera containing that music.

"You have big hair," he observed to Annie then, cocking his head this way and that to get just the right angle in studying its huge contours. "Does it hurt?"

"No."

"Does your boyfriend like it?"

"I don't have a boyfriend."

He nodded his head, as if that was a given. "A man couldn't get close enough to kiss you. Or other things," he noted, jiggling his eyebrows at her.

The man was going to hate himself tomorrow if he remembered any of this.

Annie already hated herself . . . because, for some reason, the word "kiss" coming from his lips *Who knew they would be so full and sensual when not pressed together into a thin line of disapproval?* prompted all kinds of erotic images to flicker in her underused libido. She pressed a palm to her forehead. "Boy, is it hot in here!"

"I'll second that. I'm burning up." Clay twisted his head from side to side, massaging the nape of his neck with one hand. Then, before she could protest, he loosened the string tie at the back of his shoulders and let his hospital gown slide to the floor. He wore nothing but a pair of boring white boxer shorts.

Boring, hell! He is sexy as sin.

Annie's mouth gaped open and her temperature shot up another notch or two at all that skin. And muscle. And dark silky hair.

Funny how hair on Frankie Wilks seemed repulsive. But with this man, she had to practically hold her hand back for fear she'd run her fingertips through his chest hairs. Or forearm hairs. Or . . . *Lordy, Lordy* . . . thigh hairs.

How could a man so stodgy and mean be so primitively attractive? She'd gotten to know just how stodgy and mean he could be on the ride over here. And how did a man who presumably worked at a desk all day long maintain such a flat, muscle-planed stomach?

Startled, she clicked her jaw shut.

"It's not warm in here," the doctor pointed out, intruding into her thoughts. *Thank God!* "Perhaps you both have a fever. But no, I checked your temperature, Mr. Jessup. It's normal."

Normal? There's nothing normal about the steam heat rising in this room.

Clay glared at Annie accusingly. Was he going to blame her for a fever, too? To her horror, he broke out with the husky, intimate lyrics, "You give me fever." He was staring at her the whole time.

Oh, mercy! Who would have thought he even knew an Elvis lyric? It had probably seeped into his unconscious over the years through some sort of Muzak osmosis.

"The medication will wear off in a couple of hours," the doctor was saying. "After that, we'll switch to Tylenol with Codeine. Considering his reaction, I would suggest you give him only half a tablet."

"Me? Me?" *Hey, I've got to get back to the Nativity scene. Without my supervision, who knows what my brothers are doing? Probably a hip hop version of*

"Away In a Manger." Not that my brothers know what hip hop is, aside from music videos . I wouldn't put it past Roy and Hank to be flirting with passersby, too.

The doctor finished wrapping Clay's sprained ankle tightly and took on what he'd probably practiced in front of a mirror as a serious medical demeanor. "The goose egg on the back of your head is just a hard knock, but you should be watched closely for the next twenty-four hours. I don't like the way you reacted to Darvon. Do you have family nearby to keep an eye on you?"

"I have no family," Clay declared woefully.

He's not married. Annie did a mental high five, though why she couldn't imagine. Her heart would have gone out to the man at that poignant comment if it weren't for the fact he was back to glowering at her. She tried to understand why he directed all his hostility toward her. No doubt it stemmed from the fact that he'd been *really* angry about the accident and blamed it all on her family. "You and your crazy brothers are going to pay," he'd informed her repeatedly on the drive to the hospital, during the long wait in the emergency room, throughout the examination, right up until the pain killers had performed their miraculous transformation. Good thing she'd talked her brothers into manning the Nativity scene, minus a Blessed Virgin, till she returned. They would have belted Clay for his surliness!

She was hoping he'd meant the threat figuratively. She was hoping it had only been the pain speaking. She was hoping God listened to the prayers of Blessed Mother impersonators.

They couldn't afford a new barn roof *and* a law suit.

"Well, then, perhaps we should admit you," the doctor told him. "At least overnight . . . for observation."

"I'm going back to my hotel room," Clay argued, shimmying forward to get off the examining table and stand. In the process, his boxers rode high, giving Annie an eyeful, from the side, of a tight buttock.

And her temperature cranked up another notch.

Who knew! Who could have guessed?

Ouch," he groaned as his feet hit the floor. He staggered woozily and braced himself against the wall.

"You could stay at the farm with us for a few days," Annie surprised herself by offering. The fever that had overcome her on first viewing this infuriating tyrant must have gone to her brain. "Aunt Liza can help care for you . . . " *while we're in the city doing our Nativity scene.* "It'll be more comfortable than a hotel room . . . " *and you wouldn't see us on your property.*

"That's a good idea," the doctor offered, obviously anxious to end this case and move on to the next cubicle.

"Okie dokie," Clay slurred out, the time-release medication apparently kicking in again. He was leaning against the wall, bemusedly rubbing his fingertips across his lips, as if they felt numb. Then he idly scratched his stomach . . . his *flat* stomach . . . in an utterly male gesture his lordliness probably never indulged in back at the manor house.

Her heart practically stopped as the significance of his quick agreement sunk in. *Criminey! I'm bringing Donald Trump home with me. What possessed me to make such an offer? My brothers will kill me. But, no. It really is a good idea. Get him on home turf where we can talk down his anger. Perhaps convince him to let us continue our Nativity scene the rest of the week. Take advantage of his weakened state. Heck, we might even persuade him to change his plans about razing the hotel.*

On the other hand, Elvis might be alive and living in the refrigerator at Pizza Hut.

"A farm? I've never been on a real farm before." A grin tugged at his frowning lips and he winked at her. "Eeii, eeii, oh, Daisy Mae."

Holy Cow! The grin, combined with the sexy wink, kicked up the heat in her already feverish body another notch. Even worse, the man must have a sense of humor buried under all that starch. It just wasn't fair. Annie didn't stand a chance.

"Uh-oh." His brow creased with sudden worry. "Do you have outhouses? I don't think I want to live on a farm if I have to use an outhouse."

Live? Who said anything about "live?" We're talking visit here. A day . . . two at the most. But Annie couldn't help but smile at his silly concern.

"Hey, you're not so bad looking when you smile." Clay cocked his head to one side, studying her.

"Thanks a bunch, your smoothness," she retorted. "And, no, we don't have outhouses."

"Do you have cows and horses and chickens and stuff?" he asked with a boyish enthusiasm he probably hadn't exhibited in twenty-five years . . . if ever.

"Yep. Even a goat."

"Oh, boy!" he said.

As the implications of her impetuous offer hit Annie . . . *Mr. GQ Wall Street on their humble farm* . . . she echoed his sentiment, *Oh, boy!*

"Did you ever make love in a hayloft?" he asked bluntly.

"No!" She lifted her chin indignantly, appalled that he would even ask her such an intimate question. Despite her indignation, though, unwelcome images flickered into Annie's brain, and her fever flared into a full-blown inferno.

"Neither have I," Clay noted, as he stared her straight in the eye and let loose with the slowest, sexiest grin she'd seen since Elvis died.

Who knew Scrooge could be so hot! . . .

At the sign, "Sweet Hollow Farm," Annie swerved the pickup truck off the highway and onto the washboard-rough dirt lane that meandered for a quarter mile up to the house.

Tears filled her eyes on viewing her property, as they often did when she'd been away, even if only for a few hours. She loved this land . . . the smell of its rich soil, the feel of the breeze coming off the Mississippi River, the taste of its wholesome bounty. It had been a real struggle these past ten years, but she prided herself on not having sold off even one parcel from the 120-acre family legacy.

"Oh, darn!" she muttered when she hit one of the many potholes. The eight-year-old vehicle, with its virtually nonexistent springs, went up in the air and down hard.

She worriedly contemplated her sleeping passenger who groaned, then rubbed the back of his aching head. His eyelids drifted open slowly, and Annie could see the disorientation hazing their deep blue depths. As his brain slowly cleared, he sat straighter and glanced to the pasture on the right where sixty milk cows, bearing the traditional black and white markings of the Holstein breed, grazed contentedly, along with an equal number of heifers and a half dozen new calves.

"Holy hell!" Clay muttered. "Cows!"

Geez! You'd think they didn't have dairy herds in New Jersey.

Slowly, his head turned forward, taking in the clapboard farmhouse up ahead, which must be a stark contrast to his own Princeton home. She knew she was correct in her assessment when he murmured, "The Waltons! I've landed in John Boy Central."

His slow survey continued, now to the left, where he flinched visibly on seeing her . . . still adorned in all her Priscilla/Madonna garishness.

His forehead furrowing with confusion, he loosened his tie and unbuttoned the top button of his dress shirt. Then, his fingers fluttered in an unconscious sweep down his body, hesitating for the briefest second over his groin.

Annie understood his bewilderment, even if he didn't. For some reason, an odd heat—of an erotic nature, not the body temperature type—was generated when they were in each other's presence. She empathized with his consternation. Clayton Jessup, III was a gorgeous hunk . . . when he wasn't frowning, that is. He would find it unbelievable that he could be attracted to a tasteless caricature of the Virgin Mary.

"Can you turn down the heat?" he asked testily.

"There is no heat. The thermostat broke last winter."

"Humph!" he commented as he rolled down the window on his side. "Pee-yew!" He immediately rolled it back up. "How can you stand that smell?"

"What smell? Oh, you mean the cows." She shrugged. "You get used to it after a while. Actually, I like the scent. It spells good country living to me."

"Humph! It spells cow crap to me."

Clay's condescending attitude was starting to irk Annie. She had liked him a whole lot better when he was under the influence.

"Am I being kidnapped?" he inquired hesitantly.

"Wha-at?" *Where did that insane idea come from? Oh, I see.* His gaze riveted now behind his head where Chet's hunting rifle rested in the gun rack above the bench seat. "Of course not."

"Where am I?"

"Don't you remember? You fell outside the hotel. I took you to the hospital emergency room. Oh, don't look so alarmed. You just have a sprained ankle and a goose egg on your head. The doctor said you need special care for a day or two because of the reaction you had to the Darvon, and I offered to bring you out to the farm. We're about a half hour outside Memphis."

"I agreed to stay on a . . . *farm?*" His eyes, which were really quite beautiful—a deep blue framed by thick black lashes—went wide with disbelief.

"Yes," she said in a voice stiff with affront.

"Why, for heaven's sake?"

Yep, his superiority complex was annoying the heck out of her. "Maybe because you were under the influence of drugs."

"I don't take drugs."

"You did today, buddy."

"Take me back to the hotel."

She let loose with a long sigh. "We've already been through this before. You need special care. Since you have no family, I volunteered . . . out of the goodness of my heart, I might add . . . and do I get any thanks? No, sirree."

"Who said I have no family?"

"You did?"

"I . . . did . . . not!" His face flushed with embarrassment.

Geez, why would he be uncomfortable over revealing that he had no family? It only made him appear human. Hah! Maybe that was the key. He didn't want to be human.

"I don't discuss my personal life with . . . strangers."

Bingo! "Well, you did this time."

His eyelids fluttered with sleepiness even as he spoke. "What elsh did I saaaay?"

The little demons on the wrong side of Annie's brain did a victory dance at Clay's question. Here was the perfect opportunity for her to get even for his patronizing comments.

"Well, you did a lot of singing."

His eyes shot open. "Me? In public?"

"Hmmm. Do you consider the emergency room a public place?"

"That's impossible."

"And, of course, there was your remark about haylofts . . . "

"Huh?"

Annie could see the poor guy was fighting sleep. Still, she couldn't help herself from adding, " . . . and making love."

"Making love in a hayloft? I said *that?*" Clay murmured skeptically. "With *you?* Humph! I couldn't have been *that* much out of my mind."

Before she could correct his misconception that he'd associated making love in a hayloft with her, his head fell back. Good thing, too, because Annie was about to give him a matching goose egg on the other side of his insulting noggin. "Did you say humbug?"

"No! Why does everyone think I'm a Scrooge?" he asked drowsily, followed by a lusty yawn.

"Maybe because you are."

"I said humph," he mumbled in his sleep. Then a small snore escaped from his parted lips

"Humph you, you egotistical bozo."

Can't help falling in love...

Clay awakened groggily from a deep sleep to find it was dark outside. He must have slept a good four hours or more.

For several moments, he didn't move from his position on the high, maple, poster bed, where he lay on his stomach, presumably to protect the back of his aching head. He burrowed deeper beneath the warm cocoon of a homemade patchwork quilt and smiled to himself. *So, this is how it feels to be one of the Waltons.*

By the light of a bedside hurricane lamp, he studied his surroundings. It was a cozy room, with its slanted, dormer ceiling . . . hardly bigger than his walk-in closet at home. The only furniture, besides the bed, was a matching maple dresser and a blanket chest under the low double windows facing the front of the house. A well-worn easy chair of faded blue upholstery sat in one corner, flanked on one side by a floor lamp and on the other by a small side table on which sat a paperback book and a pile of magazines. A few photographs, which he couldn't decipher from here, a high school pennant, and some cheaply framed prints of cows—*What else!*—adorned the pink rose-papered walls.

It had to belong to the Blessed Virgin Bimbo who'd brought him here. Unless the collection of Teddy Bears on the chest and the sweet-smelling toiletries on the bureau belonged to one of her brothers. Somehow, though, he didn't think any of the virile young men he'd seen in that wacky Nativity scene were gay farmers.

Clay should have felt outrage at finding himself in this predicament. Instead, a strange sense of well-being filled him, as if he'd been running a marathon for a long, long time, and finally he'd reached the finish line.

Slowly he came fully awake as the sounds of the house, which had been deathly quiet before, seeped into his consciousness. The slamming of a door. The clomp, clomp, clomp of boots on hardwood floors. Laughter and male voices. Water running. The never-ending blare of Elvis music, "You ain't nothin' but a hound dog . . . " *Good Lord! People have the nerve to call that caterwauling music. Humph!*

The cry of a baby emerged from down the hall . . . from one of the other second floor bedrooms, he presumed—mixed with the soft crooning voice of an adult male, a mixture of lullaby and words of comfort. "Shhh, Jason. You've had a long day. What a good boy you were! Just let me finish with this diaper, then you can have your bottle. Aaah, I know, I know. You're sleepy." Gradually, the crying died down to a slow whimper, then silence, except for the creak, creak, creak of a rocker.

From the deep recesses of Clay's memory, an image emerged . . . flickering and ethereal. A woman sitting in a high-backed rocking chair, holding an infant in her tender embrace. He even imagined the scent of baby powder mixed with a flowery substance. Perfume? The woman was singing a sweet, silly song to the baby about a Sandman coming with his bag of magic sleepy-time dust.

A lump formed in Clay's throat, and he could barely breathe.

Could it have been his mother . . . and him? No! His mother had left when he was barely one year old . . . and died not that long after. It was impossible that he could recall something from that age. Wasn't it?

With a snort of disgust, Clay tossed the quilt aside and sat up on the edge of the bed. He gritted his teeth to fight off the wooziness that accompanied waves of pain assaulting him from the back of his head and his bandaged ankle. Once the worst of the pain passed, he took in the fact that he was clothed only in boxers. Had he undressed himself? No, it had been the woman, Annie Fallon, and her Aunt Liza, a wiry, ancient version of the grandma on the Waltons. *God, I've got a thing about the Waltons today.* They'd helped him remove his clothing, then encouraged him to take a half pill before tucking him into the big bed.

In fact, Clay had a distinct recollection of the old buzzard eyeballing his near nude body, cackling her appreciation, then telling Annie, "Not bad for a city slicker!"

He also had a distinct recollection of Annie's response. "Don't go there, Aunt Liza. He's an egotistical bozo with ice in his veins and a Scrooge personality disorder."

"Scrooge-smoodge. You could melt him down, sweetie. Might be a nifty idea for our Christmas good deed this year."

Annie had giggled. "I can see it now. The Fallon Family Christmas Good Deed 2011: Bring a Scrooge Home for the Holidays."

I am not a Scrooge. Not, not, not! I'm not icy, either. In fact, I'm hot, hot, hot . . . at least when the Tennessee Tart is around. Furthermore, nobody . . . especially not a bunch of hayseed farmers . . . better make me their good deed. I am not a pity case.

Clay wanted nothing more than to be back home where his life was orderly and sane. He was going to sue the pants off these crackpots, but he had more important things on his mind right now. An empty stomach—which rumbled at the delicious scents wafting up from downstairs—and a full bladder.

First things first. Clay pulled on his suit pants, gingerly, and made his way into the hall, using one crutch as a prop to avoid putting full weight on his injured ankle. Across the corridor, a boy of about thirteen . . . the one who'd been a shepherd in the Nativity scene . . . was propped against the pillows on one of the twin beds in the room, reading a biology book and writing in a class notebook. He wore jeans and a tee shirt that proclaimed, "Farmers Have Long Hoes." His hair was wet from a recent shower and no longer sported the high pouf on top or duck's ass in the back. The stereo to the side of his bed blared out the Elvis music he'd heard earlier.

When he noticed Clay in the doorway, the boy set his school books aside and turned down the volume. "You're up. Finally."

"Where's the bathroom?"

"Gotta take a leak, huh?" the boy inquired crudely. "My name's Johnny," he informed him cheerily. "You're Clay, right? Annie says you're gonna stay with us for a while. Cool. Do you like Elvis?" The boy never waited for answers to his questions, just chattered away as he led the way to the end of the hall.

By the time they got there, Clay was practically crossing his legs . . . not an easy feat when walking with a sprained ankle. Was there only one bathroom to serve more than a half dozen people? There were eight bathrooms in his home, and he was the sole inhabitant these days, except for the cook and gardener, Doris and George, and they lived over the old carriage house.

Clay soon found himself in the small bathroom with an old-fashioned claw-footed tub and pedestal porcelain sink. No shower stall here, just a showerhead and plastic curtain that hung from an oval aluminum rod, suspended from the ceiling and surrounding the tub on all sides. At least there was a toilet, Clay thought, releasing a long sigh of near ecstasy after relieving himself. He'd barely zipped up his pants and washed his hands when there was a knock on the door. "You decent?" a male voice called out.

Define decent. Hobbling around barefooted, decent? Wearing nothing but a knot on my head the size of a fist and a pair of wrinkled slacks, decent? Caught practically mid-leak, decent? Under the influence of drugs, decent? "Yeah, I'm decent."

The door creaked open and the oldest brother, the father of the baby, stuck his head inside. He apparently hadn't showered yet because he still had the Elvis hair-do, though the St. Joseph outfit was gone in favor of jeans and a sweatshirt. "Hi. My name's Chet. Annie told me to give you these." He shoved a pair of jeans, white undershirt, blue plaid flannel shirt, socks and raggedy sneakers at him. "You look about the same size as me."

Clay took the items hesitantly. He was about to tell him that he wouldn't need them since he intended to go back to the hotel, asap, and call his lawyer. Before he could speak, though, the man . . . about twenty-five years old . . . asked with genuine concern, "How ya feelin'?

Your body must feel like a bulldozer ran over it."

"Do you mean your sister?"

Chet threw his head back and laughed. "Annie does have that effect sometimes, doesn't she? No, I meant the boink to your head and your twisted ankle."

Clay shrugged. "I'll be all right."

Just then Clay noticed the black satin bra hanging on the doorknob. The cups were full and enticingly feminine. He was pretty sure the wispy undergarment didn't belong to Aunt Liza. Hmmm. It would seem the scarecrow Madonna was hiding something under her virgin robes.

"Hey, that's my sister you're having indecent thoughts about," Chet protested, interrupting his reverie.

"I was not," Clay lied, hoping his flushed face didn't betray him.

"Yeah, right. Anyhow, dinner's almost ready. Do you want me to bring a tray upstairs? Or can you make it downstairs?"

Clay debated briefly whether to eat here or wait till he got back to the hotel. The embarrassing rumble in his gut decided for him. Clay told him he'd be down shortly and went back to the bedroom to change clothes while Chet made use of the shower.

A short time later, he sat at the huge oak trestle table in the kitchen waiting for Annie to come in from the barn with two of her brothers, Roy, a twenty-two-year-old vet student, and Hank, a high school senior. They were completing the second milking of the day for the dairy herd. All this information was relayed by Aunt Liza. That's what the woman had demanded that he call her after he'd addressed her as "ma'am" one too many times.

Had he ever eaten dinner in a kitchen? He didn't think so.

Did he have a personal acquaintance with anyone who had ever milked a cow? He was fairly certain he didn't.

Aunt Liza wore an apron that fit over her shoulders and hung to her knees where flesh-covered support hose bagged conspicuously under her housedress. She hustled about the commercial size stove off to one side of the kitchen. Sitting on benches that lined both sides of the table, chatting amiably with him as if it were perfectly normal for him to be there, were Chet, Johnny, whom he already met, and Jerry Lee, a fifteen-year-old. This family bred kids like rabbits, apparently. The baby was up in his crib, down for the night, Chet said hopefully.

A radio sitting on a counter was set on a twenty-four hour country music station. *Surprise, surprise.*

"Do you people honestly like that music?" Clay asked. It was probably a rude question to ask when he was in someone else's home, but he really would like to understand the attraction this crap held for the masses.

"Yeah," Chet, Jerry Lee, Johnny, and Aunt Liza said as one.

"But it's so . . . so hokey," Clay argued. "Listen to that one. `I Changed Her Oil, She Changed My Life'."

They all laughed.

"That's just it. Country music makes you feel good. You could be in a funky mood, and it makes you smile." Jerry Lee thought about what he'd said for a moment, then chuckled. "One of my favorites is `She Got the Ring, I Got the Finger'."

"Jerry Lee Fallon, I told you about using such vulgarities in this house," Aunt Liza admonished. Then she chuckled, too. "I'm partial to `You Done Tore Out My Heart and Stomped That Sucker Flat'."

"I like `I Would Have Wrote You a Letter But I Couldn't Spell Yuck'," Johnny said.

"Well, the all-time best one," Chet offered, "is `Get Your Tongue Outta My Mouth 'Cause I'm Kissing You Good-Bye'."

Some of the other titles tossed out then by one Fallon family member after another were: "How Can I Miss You If You Won't Go Away," "I've Been Flushed From the Bathroom Of Your Heart," "If I Can't Be Number One In Your Life, Then Number Two On You," "You Can't Have Your Cake and Edith Too," and the one they all agreed was best, "I Shaved My Legs For *This*?"

Despite himself, Clay found himself laughing with the whole crazy bunch.

Just then, the back door could be heard opening onto a mudroom. Voices rang out with teasing banter.

"You better not have mooned any passersby, Hank? That's all we need is a police citation on top of everything else," Annie was chastising her brother.

"I didn't say he mooned the girl," another male said. It must be Roy, the vet student. "I said he was mooning *over* her."

There was the sound of laughter then and running water as they presumably washed their hands in a utility sink.

Seconds later, two males entered the room, rubbing their hands briskly against the outside chill which they carried in with them. They nodded at him in greeting and sat down on the benches, maneuvering their long legs awkwardly under the table.

Only then did Clay notice the woman who stepped through the

doorway. She was tall and thin. Her long, *long* legs that went from here to the Texas Panhandle were encased in soft, faded jeans, which were tucked into a pair of work boots. An oversized denim shirt . . . probably belonging to one of her brothers . . . covered her on the top, hanging down to her knees with sleeves rolled up to the elbows. A swath of sandy brunette hair laid straight and thick to her shoulders. Not a lick of make-up covered her clear complexion. Even so, her lips were full . . . almost too full for her thin face . . . and parted over large, even white teeth. She resembled a thinner, younger, more beautiful version of Julia Roberts.

Clay put his forehead down on the table and groaned.

He knew everyone was probably gawking at him as if he'd lost his mind, but he couldn't help himself. He knew even before the fever flooded his face and arms and legs and that particular hot zone in between . . . he knew exactly who this stranger was. It was, unbelievably, Annie Fallon.

He cracked his eyes open a bit, still with his face in his plate, and glanced sideways at her where she still stood, equally stunned, in the doorway. Neither of them seemed to notice the hooting voices surrounding them.

How could he have been so blind?

How could he not have seen what was happening here?

How could he not have listened to the cautionary voice of the bellhop who'd warned of destiny and God's big toe?

All the pieces fit together now in the puzzle that had plagued Clay since he'd arrived in Memphis. God's big toe had apparently delivered him a holy kick in the ass. Not to mention the fever He'd apparently sent to thaw his icy heart.

Clay, a sophisticated, wealthy venture capitalist, was falling head over heels in love at first sight with a farmer. Old McAnnie.

Donald Trump and Daisy Mae.

Hell! It will never work.

Will it?

He raised his head and took a longer look at the woman who was frozen in place, staring at him with equal incredulity. It was a sign of the madness that had overcome them both that the laughter rippling around them failed to penetrate their numbed consciousnesses.

He knew for sure that he was lost when a traitorous thought slipped out, and he actually spoke it aloud.

"Where's the hayloft, honey?"

Chapter Three

A smart man isn't above a little subterfuge...

Clay felt as if he'd landed smack dab in the middle of the Mad Hatter's party. It was debatable who was the mad one, though . . . him or the rest of the inmates in this bucolic asylum.

Love? Me? Impossible!

Elvis music blared in the background—*ironically, "Can't Help Falling in Love With You"*—and everyone talked at once, each louder than the other in order to be heard. A half-dozen strains of dialogue were going on simultaneously, but no one seemed to notice. Good thing, too. It gave him a chance to speculate in private over his monumental discovery of just a few moments ago.

I'm falling in love.

Impossible! Uh-uh, none of this falling business for me.

What other explanation is there for this fever that overtakes me every time I look at her? And, man, she is so beautiful. Well, not beautiful. Just perfect. Well, not perfect-perfect. Hell, the woman makes my knees sweat, just looking at her.

Maybe it's not love. I've never been in love before. How do I know it's love? Maybe it's just lust.

Love, lust, whatever. I'm a goner.

But a farmer? A farmer?

"How come you and Annie keep googley-eying each other?" Johnny asked.

"Shut your teeth and eat," Aunt Liza responded, whacking Johnny on the shoulder with a long-handled wooden spoon.

"Ouch!"

Meantime, a myriad of platters and bowls were being set on the table. And Aunt Liza assured him this was an everyday meal, no special spread on his behalf.

Pot roast (about ten pounds, give or take a hind quarter) cut into half-inch slabs. Mashed potatoes. Gravy. Thick noodles cooked in beef broth. Creamed spinach. Pickled beets. Succotash (*Whatever the hell that was!*). Chow-chow (*Whatever the hell that was, too!*). Tossed salad. Coleslaw. Homemade biscuits and butter. Pitchers of cold, unhomogenized milk at either end of the table sporting a two-inch header of real cream. Canned pears. Chocolate layer cake and vanilla ice cream.

There were enough calories and fat grams on this table to fatten up the entire nation of Bosnia. Yet, amazingly, everyone here was whip-thin. Either they'd all inherited good genetic metabolisms, or they engaged in a massive amount of physical labor. He suspected it was a combination of both.

"Do you think it's a good idea to eat so much red meat and dairy?" Clay made the mistake of inquiring.

"Bite your tongue," everyone declared at once.

For a moment, Clay had forgotten that these were dairy farmers whose livelihood depended on milk products. Plus, they had about a hundred thousand pounds of beef on the hoof in their own backyard.

Clay rubbed a forefinger over his upper lip, pondering all that had happened to him so far this day. In the midst of the conversations swirling around him now, he felt as if he was having a personal epiphany. Not just the monumental discovery that, for the first time in his life, he was falling in love. It was much more than that. He never realized till this moment how much he'd missed having a family. He never would have described himself as a lonely man—loner, perhaps, but not *lonely*. Now, he knew that he'd been lonely for a long time.

And that wacky bellhop had been right this morning about his coldness. Over the years, he must have built up an icy crust around his heart. *Just like my father.* Little by little, it was melting now. Every time he came within a few feet of Annie, the strange fever enveloped him, and his chest tightened with emotions too new to understand. He yearned so much. For what exactly, he didn't know.

In a daze, he reached for a biscuit, but Chet coughed meaningfully and Aunt Liza glared stonily at him. Once he sheepishly put the roll back, Annie took his hand on the one side, and Jerry Lee on the other. All around the table, everyone bowed their heads and joined hands, including Aunt Liza and Chet who sat in the end chairs, on either side. Then Annie said softly, "Lord, bless this food and all the poor people in the world who have less than we do, even the rich people who have less than we do. For this bounty, we give you thanks. Amen."

Everyone dug in heartily then, passing the bowls and platters around the table as they chattered away. Clay soon found himself with an unbelievable amount of high cholesterol food on his plate, and enjoying it immensely. He practically sighed at the almost sinful flavor of melt-in-your-mouth potatoes mixing on his palate with rich beef gravy.

"Frankie Wilks called when you were in the barn." Jerry Lee bobbed his eyebrows at Annie. "Said something about wantin' you to go to the Christmas Eve candlelight service with him."

"Oooooh! Oooooh!" several of her brothers taunted, meanwhile shoveling down food like monks after a Lent-long fast.

"Who's Frankie Wilks?" Clay's voice rose with more consternation than he had any right to exhibit. *Yet.*

"The milkman," Annie said, scowling at Jerry Lee. She had a hearty appetite, too, Clay noticed, though you wouldn't know it from her thin frame. Probably came from riding herd on her cows.

Did they ride herd on cows?

Then Annie's words sank in. *The milkman? The milkman? I have a fifty million dollar portfolio, I'm not a bad looking guy, attracting women has never been a problem for me, and my competition is . . . a milkman?*

Competition? Whoa! Slow down this runaway testosterone train.

"Don't you be sittin' there, gloatin' like a pig in heat, Chet," Aunt Liza interjected as she put another slab of beef onto Clay's plate, despite his raised hand of protest. His mouth was too full to speak. "You got a phone call today, too, Chet."

Everyone at the table turned in tandem to stare at Chet.

"Emmy Lou? Right?" Chet didn't appear very happy as he asked the question.

"Yep. She was callin' from London. Said she won't be home before Christmas to pick up the baby, after all."

"Stupid damn girl," Annie cursed under her breath. Clay suspected *damn* was not a word she used lightly.

"You drove her away, if you ask me," Hank accused, reaching for his dessert, which Aunt Liza shoved out of the way, pushing more salad his way first."

"Who asked you, mush-for-brains?" Chet snapped.

"All you had to do was tell her you love her," Roy teased. He waved a forkful of potatoes in the air as he spoke.

"I offered to marry her, didn't I?"

"*Offered?* Sometimes, Chet, you are dumber than pig spit," Annie remarked. "Have some pickled beets," she added as an aside to Clay.

Chet's face, which was solemn to begin with, went rigid with anger, but he said nothing.

"Is this Lilith?" Annie addressed Aunt Liza as she chewed on a bite of pot roast.

"Yep. Nice and tender, ain't she?" Aunt Liza answered. "Thank

God we got rid of the last of Alicia in the stew Friday night. She was tough as cow hide."

They name the cows they eat? Will they eat those two sheep that were in the Nativity scene, too? Or . . . God forbid . . . the donkey? Bile rose in Clay's throat, and he discreetly pushed the remainder of his pot roast to the side of the plate.

"Speaking of cows, I noticed this morning that Mirabelle's vulva is swollen and red," Johnny interjected. "We better breed her soon."

"I'll do it tomorrow night," Annie said.

Clay choked on the pot roast still remaining in his mouth. A thirteen-year-old kid was discussing vulvae at the dinner table, and no one blinked an eye. Even worse, Annie . . . *his* Annie . . . was going to breed a cow. "Can I watch?"

"Huh? Oh, sure," she said and resumed eating. Clay liked to watch Annie eat. Her full lips moved sensuously as she relished each morsel, no matter if it was a beet or the chocolate cake. He about lost it when her tongue darted out to lick a speck of chocolate icing off the edge of her bottom lip. "If you're sure you want to. Some people get kind of squeamish."

"I can handle it," he asserted. Heck, he'd probably seen worse in Grand Central Station. But, hot damn, Annie had just-like-that agreed to let him observe her breeding a cow. And she wasn't even embarrassed.

"Are you rich?" Roy asked.

"Roy!" Annie and Aunt Liza chastised.

"Yes."

"Yes?" Everyone at the table put down their eating utensils and gaped at him. Except Annie. Her face fell in disappointment. Was she falling in love with him, too? He didn't have time to ponder for long why his being rich was a disadvantage. He just kicked into damage control. "Well, not *rich*-rich."

"How rich?" Annie demanded to know.

Before he could respond, Hank commented, "Betcha draw a bunch of chicks, having heaps of money and all."

"At least a bunch," Clay said dryly.

Annie flashed Hank a glower that the kid ignored, smiling widely. "Man, if I had a little extra cash, and a hot car, I would be the biggest chick magnet in the whole U-ni-ted States. I'm already the best in the South."

His brothers hooted their opinion of his high self-opinion.

"If you'd get your mind off the girls once in a while," Aunt Liza reprimanded, "maybe you'd pass that Cow-cue-lust."

Everyone laughed at her mispronunciation of the word calculus, except Annie. "And, by the way, where is your second term report card, Mr. I-Am-The-Stud?"

"Uh-oh," Johnny and Jerry Lee groaned at the same time. "You had to remind her."

Clay's lips twitched with suppressed mirth. Being in a family was kind of fun.

But Jerry Lee was back on his case again. "Do you have a chauffeur?"

Clay felt his face turn red. "Benson . . .George Benson . . . doubles as my *driver* and gardener. His wife Doris is my cook and housekeeper."

"You have a gardener!" Annie wailed. You'd think he had told her he employed an ax murderer. "And a housekeeper!"

"Do you live in a mansion?" Johnny's young face was rapt with interest.

"No, he lives in a trailer, you dweeb," Hank remarked, nudging Johnny in the ribs with an elbow.

"No. Definitely not. Uh-uh. I do *not* live in a mansion." This was the most incredible conversation Clay had ever experienced. Why was he trying to downplay his lifestyle?

To make Annie more comfortable, that was why.

Annie's eyes narrowed. "How big is this non-mansion?"

"Tweytfllrms," he mumbled.

"What?"

"Twenty-two rooms. But it's not a mansion."

"Twenty-two rooms! And you live there alone?" She appeared as if she might cry. "You probably have caviar for breakfast."

He shook his head quickly. "Toast, fresh squeezed orange juice and black coffee, that's what I have. Every day. I don't even like caviar."

"—gold faucets in your bathrooms and—"

"They're only gold-plated. Cheap gold-plating. And brass. I'm pretty sure some of them are brass."

"—and date movie stars—"

"The only movie star I ever dated was Natalie Portman, and that was before she was famous, when we were both students at Harvard. Her name was Natalie Hershlag. And it wasn't really a date, just brunch at—"

"Natalie Portman!" five males at the table exclaimed.

Annie honed in on another irrelevant fact. "He eats brunch. *Brunch.*

Oh, God! He must think he's landed on Welfare Row. *Better Homes and Slums.*"

"Who's Natalie Portman?" Aunt Liza wanted to know. "Is she one of those "Desperate Housewives" hussies Roy watches all the time?"

Before anyone could explain, Annie sighed loudly and declared, "Maybe I better take you back to your hotel tonight."

"An-nie!" Johnny whined. "You promised we would put up the Christmas tree tonight."

"Yeah, Annie," Jerry Lee chimed in. "We would have had it up by now if it wasn't for your dumb Nativity scene idea."

"Well, actually . . . uh, I'm not feeling so good," Clay surprised himself by saying. He was in a sudden panic. If he went back to the hotel, he'd have no opportunity to study this fever thing with Annie . . . or this falling in . . . uh, whatever. He could easily conduct business on his cell phone and iPad from the farm, for a day or two anyhow.

"You aren't?" Annie was immediately concerned.

"Maybe coming downstairs was too much for you." Aunt Liza got up and walked to his end of the table, then put a hand to his forehead to check his temperature. "Yep, he's got a fever."

No kidding! What else is new?

"I'll help you back up the steps," Chet offered.

"No, that's all right. I think I could sit in a chair and watch you put up your tree." *I am shameless. Pathetic, even.* Then, before he had a chance to bite his tongue, he blurted out, "I've never had a Christmas tree."

Everyone stared at him as if he'd just arrived from Mars. Or New Jersey.

"My father didn't believe in commercial holidays," he disclosed, a defensive edge to his voice. *Put a zipper on it, Jessup. You don't want pity. You want . . . well, something else.*

"That settles it, then," Aunt Liza said, tears welling in her eyes.

Yep, pity.

Annie reached under the table and took his hand in hers.

On the other hand, I can stomach a little pity. Immediately, a warm feeling of absolute rightness filled him almost to overflowing. He knew then that he'd made the right decision forestalling his return to the city. Besides, he'd just remembered something important.

He hadn't checked out the hayloft yet.

Getting into the Christmas spirit...

Annie had thought she was drowning in troubles this morning before she ever left for Memphis. Little had she known that her troubles would quadruple by nightfall.

In fact, she'd brought trouble home with her, willingly, and it sat big as you please right now on her living room sofa, with one extended leg propped up on an ottoman, gazing at her with smoldering eyes that promised . . . well, trouble.

Clayton Jessup, III had looked handsome this morning when Annie had seen him for the first time in his cashmere overcoat and custom-made suit. But now, sporting a nighttime shadow of whiskers, dressed in tight, faded jeans, a white tee shirt and an unbuttoned blue plaid flannel shirt that brought out the midnight blue of his eyes, the man was drop-dead gorgeous, testosterone-oozing, hot-hot-hot trouble-on-the-hoof, with a capitol T.

"I need to talk with you . . . *alone*," he whispered when Annie stepped close to get the popcorn and cranberry strings he'd been working on for the past two hours. When Aunt Liza had first suggested that he help make the homemade decorations, he'd revealed with an endearing bashfulness, "My father would have been appalled to see me performing this mundane chore. 'Time is money,' was his favorite motto. Over and over he used to tell me, 'You're wasting time, boy. Delegate, delegate, delegate.'" Then, Clay had ruined the effect of his shy revelation by asking Aunt Liza the crass question, "Don't you think it would be cheaper, time wise, to buy these garlands, already strung?"

Clucking with disapproval, Aunt Liza had shoved the darning needle, a ball of string and bowls of popcorn and cranberries in his lap. "You can't put a price tag on tradition, boy."

Along the same line, he'd observed, "I never realized Christmas trees could be so messy." Her brothers had just dragged in the seven-foot Blue Spruce from the porch, leaving a trail of fresh needles on the hardwood floors. "Wouldn't an artificial tree be a better investment in the long run?"

They'd all looked at him as if he'd committed some great sacrilege. Which he had, of course. An artificial tree? Never! Couldn't he smell the rich Tennessee forest in the pine scent that permeated the air? Couldn't he understand that bringing a live tree into the house was like bringing a bit of God's bounty inside, a direct link between the upcoming celebration of Christ's birth and the world's ongoing rejuvenation of life?

"Think with your heart, not your brain, sonny," Aunt Liza had urged.

Now the tree decorating was almost complete, except for the star that had been in the family for three generations, the garlands, and the last of the handcrafted ornaments made by Fallon children for the past twenty-five or so years. And all Annie could think about was the fact that the man had said he wanted to talk with her, *alone*. About two thousand red flags of warning went up in Annie's already muddled senses. "If it's about your threat to sue, well, you can see we don't have much." The Fallons were a proud family, but her brothers were trusting souls, and in the course of the evening they'd casually divulged the dire need for a new barn roof, the money crunch caused by lower milk prices, and Roy's tuition woes. They'd even discussed in length how every year at Christmastime the Fallons performed one good deed, no matter how tight they were for money. One year it had been a contribution to a local farm family whose house had burned down. Another year, they made up two dozen baskets for a food bank in Memphis, complete with fresh turkeys, home-canned fruits, vegetables and preserves, crisp apples and pure maple syrup. Still another year, when the till was bone dry, they'd donated ten hours each to Habitat for Humanity. This year, they hadn't yet come up with any ideas. But they would before Christmas Eve. Tradition demanded it.

"You can sue us if you want, but it's obvious that we barely have two dimes to spare. I'll fight you to the death if you try to take our farm."

"What in God's name gave you the idea that I want your farm?" he snapped. Then his voice lowered. "It's not your farm I'm interested in, Annie."

Annie loved the way he said her name, soft and special. But there was no way in the world she would ask what he meant by that enigmatic remark. "Perhaps we could pay for your medical expenses over a period of time."

He shook his head slowly. "I'm insured."

Okay, he's insured, but he didn't say he wouldn't sue us. Should I ask, or assume that he won't. Hmmm. Better to let sleeping dogs lie. "I hope you're not going to stop us from doing our Nativity scene for the rest of the week. You've got to know it's our last chance to earn some extra cash. And—"

He put up a halting hand. "I'd rather you didn't go back to that sideshow again, but that's not why I want to talk with you."

"It's not?" Annie's heart was beating so fast she was afraid he might hear it.

"It's not."

"What do you want from us, then?"

"From your family . . . ," he shrugged, " . . . nothing."

She reflected on his words. "From me?" she squeaked out.

A slow grin crept across his lips causing those incredible dimples to emerge. Annie had to clench her fists against the compulsion to touch each of the tiny indentations, to trace the outline of those kiss-me lips, to—

A low, masculine chuckle emerged from said lips. "If you don't stop looking at me like that, Annie-love," he said in a husky undertone, "I'll *show* you what I want."

Annie-love? Mercy! "I don't know what you mean," she said huffily and backed away before he could tell her exactly how she'd been ogling him and what he would show her.

"You know what I mean, Annie," he commented to her back. "*You know.*"

She didn't know, for sure, but her imagination kicked in big-time. It was the fever, of course—that strange malady that seemed to affect only the two of them when they were in the same room. Hadn't they complained of the heat all night? And they both knew it had nothing to do with the roaring fire in the fireplace. It was a fire of another kind entirely.

After that, in the midst of their decorating efforts, Clay helped Hank with his calculus homework. No one was surprised that a man with his financial background could actually perform the complicated equations. Then Jerry Lee expressed a curiosity about Clay's electronic planner gadget. He showed him its various gee-whiz functions and answered questions about the stock market. Annie never realized that Jerry Lee was even interested in the investment world.

Throughout the evening, Aunt Liza coddled them all by bringing out trays of hot chocolate and her latest batch of Christmas sugar cookies. "Have another," she kept urging Clay who swore his jeans were going to unsnap.

Now that was a picture Annie tried to avoid.

Finally, the tree decorating was complete.

"Turn off the lamps and flick on the tree lights," Aunt Liza advised on cue. The darkened room looked beautiful under the sheen of the multi-colored lights. There was a communal sigh of appreciation from everyone in the room, even Clay.

"Is everyone ready?" Johnny asked, reaching over to turn up the volume on the old-fashioned stereo record player. It had been pumping out Elvis Christmas songs all night.

Her family began singing "Blue Christmas" along with Elvis . . . a less than harmonic but poignant custom that always brought tears to her eyes. It reminded her of her parents, now gone, and the yuletide rituals they'd started that would be carried on by Fallons forevermore. In some ways, it was as if their parents were still with them at times like this.

Annie glanced over to Clay to see how he was reacting to what he must consider a sappy custom. By the glow of the tree lights and the burning logs in the fireplace, she noticed no condescending smirk on his face. He seemed stunned.

Moving to the front of the sofa and leaning forward, she inquired, "What do you think of your first Christmas tree?"

Before Annie could blink, he grabbed her by the wrist and pulled her down to the sofa at his side. One of her brother's chuckled mid-stanza, but Annie couldn't bother about that. Clay had tucked her close with an arm locked around her shoulders and his hip pressed tight against hers. Only then did he answer . . . a husky whisper breathed against her ear.

"This is a Christmas I will never forget, Annie-love."

She wasn't the Virgin Mary, but...

They were alone at last.

And Clay had plans.

Big plans.

Aunt Liza had gone to her bedroom on the first floor off the kitchen after wishing everyone "Merry Christmas" and giving each a goodnight kiss on the cheek, including Clay, who felt a tightening in his throat at being included in her family. Hank had put another log on the fire for them, winked, then hit the telephone for a long chat with his latest girlfriend. Roy and Jerry Lee had gone out to the barn for a final check of the farm animals. Chet was upstairs giving his baby a last night-time bottle. Johnny was probably asleep already, being among those who'd gotten up by four a.m. today to do farm chores before going into Memphis. Even Elvis had shut down for the night.

Clay turned to Annie. He relaxed the arm that had been wrapped around her shoulders, holding her immobile, and his hand crept under her silky hair to clasp the bare nape of her neck. His other hand briefly traced the line of her jaw and her full, parted lips before tunneling into her hair, grasping her scalp.

She moaned. But she didn't pull away. She, too, must sense the inevitable . . . the impending kiss, and so much more.

"Oh, Annie, I've been waiting to do this for hours."

"I've been waiting, too," she confessed, turning slightly so he could see her better. "For a long, long time."

He wasn't sure if she referred to a kiss or this bigger thing looming between them. By the expression of fear on her face, it was probably the latter. Hell, he was scared, too.

At first, he just settled his lips over hers, testing. With barely any pressure at all, he shifted from side to side till they fit perfectly. Then, deepening the kiss, he persuaded her to open for him. The first tentative thrust of his tongue inside her mouth brought stars behind his closed lids and another moan from Annie. He pulled out and whispered against her moist lips, "You taste like candy canes."

She smiled against his lips and whispered back, "You taste like popcorn. All buttery and salty and movie balcony naughty."

Chuckling, he cut her off, kissing her in earnest now. Long, drugging kisses that went on and on. He couldn't get enough. She seemed the same.

"Annie-love," he cautioned after what appeared an hour, but was probably only a few minutes. "Your brothers are back." The clomp of heavy boots could be heard on the back porch by the kitchen.

They both sat up straighter, their clasped hands the only body contact.

"G'night," Roy and Jerry Lee said as they passed through the living room on their way to the stairs. There was a snicker of amusement in Roy's tone, but thankfully he said nothing more.

"Were they kissin'?" he heard Jerry Lee ask in an undertone once they were in the upper hall.

"Do pigs grunt?" Roy answered.

"Annie? Our Annie? Yeech!"

"What? You didn't think she knew how to kiss?"

"Sure . . . I mean, I guess so. It's just . . . I never saw her lookin' so pink and flustery. And Clay, he looks guilty as sin."

"Better not be too guilty, or too sinful," Roy growled. Their muted voices faded to nothing.

Annie put her face in her hands and groaned. "Pink and flustery! I'll never hear the end of this. Never. By tomorrow morning, my brothers will be making pink jokes. What's pink and goes squawk-squawk? A flustered Annie chicken. Ha, ha, ha."

Clay barely suppressed a smile. Her embarrassment was endearing. "Annie, that's not a joke. It's not even funny."

She raised her head. "Since when do my brothers' jokes have to be funny? And don't think you're going to escape their teasing either. Uh-uh. You are in for it, big-time. How about, `What's got a scratchy jaw and googley eyes?'"

"An-nie," he warned.

"A Princeton hog in rut." At his gaping mouth, she nodded her head vigorously. "See. That's what you can expect."

Is she saying I have googley eyes . . . whatever the hell googley eyes are? Clay shuttered his lashes half-mast and pulled Annie into his embrace again, fitting her face into the curve of his neck. He kissed the top of her head, murmuring, "Oh, Annie. It doesn't matter what they say when this feels so right."

She sighed, which he took for a nonverbal sign of agreement, and nestled closer. "I suppose you want to sleep with me."

Whoa! That got his attention. "Where did that come from? We were just kissing, Annie." *Not that other parts of my body weren't headed in that direction. But talk about getting right to the point!*

Annie put her hands on his chest and shoved away slightly so she could look at him directly. "Are you saying you don't want to make love with me?"

"Hell, no. Of course I want you. . .*that way.*"

He reached for her, but she squirmed back, keeping her distance. "Me, too."

Me, too? What does that mean? Oh, my God! Did she just say she wants to make love with me? "Annie, this is going a bit fast, don't you think? I mean, I'm not sure it's a good idea making love on your living room couch where anyone could barge in at any moment." *Me, too? Son of a bitch! I do like a woman who can make up her mind. No games with my Annie. No, sirree.*

She made a snorting sound of disgust, waving a hand in the air. "That's not what I meant, you dolt."

His spirits immediately deflated. She didn't mean what he'd thought she meant. Damn!

"I'm just trying to tell you that . . . uh . . . um . . . "

"What?" he prodded. This was the most disarming, confusing conversation he'd ever had with a woman, and if it got any hotter in this room he was going to explode.

As if mirroring his thoughts, Annie wiped her forehead with the back of one hand and began to unbutton her flannel shirt, revealing a tight white tee shirt underneath.

He refused to look *there*.

He was not going to look.

He was looking.

Man, oh, man!

That had been her bra in the bathroom, all right. Her breasts pushed against the thin material, full and uptilted, the nipples puckered into hard peaks. It wasn't that she was big-busted but because she was so thin, it appeared that way. Good thing she didn't look like that in her Blessed Mother outfit or she'd have men propositioning her right there in the Nativity scene. Or else she'd get some super tips.

"Stop looking at me like that."

"Like what?" he choked out.

"Like you're . . . like you're . . . "

" . . . interested?" He couldn't stop the grin that twitched at his lips.

"Stop smirking. I'm trying to tell you something."

"Oh?" he said, trying his damnedest not to look at her chest and not to grin with pure, unadulterated anticipation. As a final measure, he clenched his fists at his side to keep from grabbing for her.

"I'm a virgin."

That was the last thing Clay had expected to hear.

"A virgin?" he squeaked out. *A twenty-eight-year-old virgin?*

"Yeah, isn't that the biggest joke of all?"

She was actually embarrassed by her virginity. Well, it did put a new light on their making love. Not that he didn't still want her, but it sure as hell wouldn't take place on a sofa with broken springs in a houseful of gun-toting brothers and an aunt who wielded a wicked spoon. "Annie, why tell me this now?"

"You have a right to know . . . if I'm reading that glimmer in your eye the right way."

You are. Clay lowered his lashes and tried his best to curb that "glimmer" in his eye.

"You probably think I'm repressed or gay or ultra-religious. But it's just that I haven't had time for dating since my parents died. And Prince Charming doesn't come riding his charger down the lane to a dairy farm real often."

"So, I'm the first prince to come your way?" he asked with a laugh.

She slanted him a "Behave Yourself" glare and went on, "Now that you know, I suppose you don't want me anymore." She glanced at him shyly and looked away.

He took her chin in his hand and turned her face back to him. Kissing her lips lightly, he murmured, "I still want you."

A slow, wicked smile spread across her lips. "Stand up, then," she ordered.

Huh? With his brow furrowing in confusion, he got up cautiously, bracing himself on one crutch. At the same time, the stereo suddenly came on with Elvis wailing, "It's Now Or Never." He jerked back at the unexpected noise and Annie laughed.

"The stereo does that sometimes. There's a short in its electric circuit, I guess."

He thought about telling her that was a safety hazard, but decided he had more important things on his mind right now. Like why she'd wanted him to stand, and why she was staring at him, arms folded across her chest, with that odd expression on her face. She was probably afraid, being a virgin and all. It was sweet of her, actually.

"Don't be afraid, Annie. I won't do anything to hurt you."

She laughed, a joyous, rippling sound mingling with Elvis's husky Now-or-Never warning.

That was probably nervous laughter, Clay concluded. Still, he tilted his head to the side, questioning. "Annie?"

"Take off your shirt, Clay. Please."

Her softly spoken words ambushed him. With a quick intake of breath, he almost swallowed his tongue.

"Reeeaal slow."

Chapter Four

What the lady wants, the lady gets . . .

Annie could see that she'd shocked Clay, but she didn't care. This was her big chance.

Just because she was a virgin didn't mean she was a dried-up old spinster with no needs. Like she'd told him before, there weren't many princes who ambled on down their farm lane. And when one not-so-perfect specimen accidentally rode in, well, heck, she'd be a fool not to drag him down off his horse and have her way with him.

"I have needs," she told him matter-of-factly.

"Needs?" he choked out. Geez, the man looked as if he was choking on his own tongue. Where was the suave, cool-as-a-hybrid-cucumber man who could cut a person off at the knees with a single icy stare?

Okay, sometimes Annie forgot that city people didn't understand the plain speaking of farm folks who lived with the facts of life on a daily basis. Those who worked with the land and animals tended to be more earthy, more accepting of the forces of nature. Sex was just another of the physical urges God gave all animals, nothing to be embarrassed about. At least, that's what she told herself. If she didn't justify her behavior in that way, she'd have to admit she was a lust-driven hussy with a compulsion to jump the poor prince's royal bones.

"Yep. Needs," she answered with more bravado than she really had. If he rejected her, she was going to crawl in a hole and never come out. "So shuck that shirt, honey. I've been having indecent thoughts ever since I saw you in the emergency room in those cute little boxer shorts."

Stains of scarlet bloomed on his face at her mention of his boxers. Or was it her needs turning up his internal thermometer?

"This is a joke, right?" Clay said, backing up a bit till his back hit the wall. He probably needed it to support his sore foot, or maybe his suddenly weak knees.

Oh, swell! I'm scaring him. Slow down, Annie. Play it cool. Pretend he's just hairy old Frankie Wilks.

Hah!

"No joke, Clay. You have a chest that would cause a cloistered nun to melt, and I already have a fever to begin with. So take off the darn shirt, for crying out loud." Her voice had turned shrill at the end.

"All right, all right," he said, raising a palm in surrender. "Let's backtrack to step one. You want me to take off my shirt because you like my chest?"

"Yes." She stood and walked slowly toward him.

He smiled then, one of those glorious deals that bared his even white teeth and caused those irresistible dimples to play peek-a-boo with her heart. "What if someone walks in . . . like your aunt?"

She pooh-poohed that idea. "Do you think Aunt Liza hasn't seen a male chest before? In a house with five males?"

"But Annie," Clay explained with exaggerated patience. "If you want me to take off my shirt, I'm pretty sure I'll be wanting you to take off your shirt." He flashed her a "So there!" grin.

"Oh." Delicious images swam in Annie's head at that suggestion. She stood several feet away from him, but she could feel his heat. "Well, I guess I forgot to mention that Aunt Liza is dead to the world once her head hits the pillow. Her alarm clock, set religiously at 4 a.m., is the only thing that will awaken her now."

"Yes, you did forget to mention that fact." His grin didn't waver at all. "And your brothers?"

"The same. Besides, there's an unwritten rule in the Fallon house. Nobody walks in unannounced on a courting couple . . . not that you and I are courting, mind you. Don't get your feathers all ruffled in that regard. I'm not out to trap you."

"My feathers aren't ruffled," he protested indignantly. Then, understanding that they wouldn't be interrupted, he immediately pulled off the flannel shirt and raised the tee shirt over his head. Superman couldn't have done it faster. After that, standing still, he waited for her to make the next move. He wasn't smiling now.

He was so beautiful. Wide shoulders. Narrow waist and hips. A thin frame, but not too thin. Muscles delineating his upper arms and forearms and the planes of his chest and abdomen—not muscle builder, puffed-up flesh, just healthy, fit male muscle. Dark silky hairs peppered his chest, leading down in a vee to the low-riding jeans.

Under her sweeping appraisal, he never once lowered his eyes. Women faltered under such close scrutiny, but not men . . . not this man.

"Can I touch you?" she whispered.

The hard ridges of his stomach muscles lurched.

Heat curled in her stomach, almost a mirroring reflection.

At first, he closed his eyes and a low strangled sound emerged from his lips. He appeared to be out of breath, panting. When he lifted his eyelids, Annie almost staggered backwards under the onslaught of the blue fire. "If you *don't* touch me, I think I'll go up in smoke," he whispered back.

Well, that sounds encouraging. She stepped closer and put her hands on his shoulders. He tried to take her in his arms, but Annie swatted his hands away. She wanted to do this herself, with no distractions. "Let me . . . I want . . . ," she murmured, her brain reeling with a feverish urgency. "I want to do things to you. So many things." *Things? What things? Where are these outlandish thoughts coming from? And how am I getting up the nerve to say them aloud?*

"Annie . . . ," he started to say, then paused, lost for words. "You take my breath away."

"Don't move," she ordered and ran her fingertips down both sides of his tension-corded neck, over his shoulders, skimming over the light furring on his arms to his hands where she twined their fingers for one brief moment, raising the knuckles of one hand, then the other for a brief kiss. She released his hands then, setting them back at his side.

Smoothing the palms of her hands across his chest, she felt his heartbeat thud. She watched in fascination as the flat male nipples hardened and elongated.

Clay gritted out one crude word between clenched teeth. Annie decided to take the expletive as a compliment.

She couldn't resist then. Lowering her head, she licked one nipple, sucked it into her mouth, rolled it between her lips.

"Omygod, omygod, omygod!" Clay exclaimed, snaking out a hand to grasp her nape, then lift her into an embrace where her hips cradled his erection. He was still braced against the wall, thank heavens! Otherwise, they would have probably fallen. Alternately kissing her with a devouring hunger and growling into the curve of her neck, he ended up cupping her buttocks and rocking her against him. All the time he was overcome with a violent shiver.

Incredibly, Annie felt herself approaching climax. It was way too soon for that, and not the way she wanted it to happen.

It was Clay who slowed the action. Setting her away from him, he said in a grainy rasp, "Do you know what I want, Annie-love?"

She cocked her head to the side. "I think so."

"Not *that*, silly girl. I mean, yes, I want *that*, but not now. What I really want is to feel your skin against mine."

It took several moments for his words to sink in. When they did, Annie felt a thrill of excitement ripple through her already oversensitized body. She jerked off her flannel shirt, then drew the tee shirt up and over her head, leaving only a plain, white nylon bra. Through its thin fabric, her small nipples stood out with stiff, pale rose peaks, aching for his touch.

His eyes studied her with apparent appreciation. He licked his lips as he waited for her final unveiling. When the wispy bra fell to the floor, his eyes seemed to water up. "Oh, Annie, you are so beautiful."

She wasn't beautiful, Annie knew that. But it was nice that he found her appealing. She wanted to be beautiful for him.

"It's your turn now, sweetheart. Don't move," he said then, giving equal attention to her body, murmuring compliments to each part examined by his tantalizing fingers and feathery kisses. When he came to her breasts, Annie's heart stood still. First he raised them up from underneath in the palms of his hands, then skimmed both nipples with the pads of his thumbs. By the time he angled his head down to wet one, then the other with his lips and tongue, and finally suckled rhythmically, Annie was mewling with an increasing frenzy.

Recognizing her spiraling passion, Clay eased away from the wall and backward toward the couch, taking Annie with him. But he lost his balance and fell onto his back, half reclining, with one leg extended out to the floor. Annie tripped, too, and ended up plopped on top of him. When she raised herself up, she found herself, amazingly, straddling him, jean-clad groin to jean-clad groin.

Clay groaned, a long, husky sound of pain emitted through clenched teeth.

Immediately, Annie remembered Clay's injuries. It was a sign of her fevered brain that she'd forgotten. "Oh, my God! Did I hurt you? Is it your head? Or your ankle?"

Clay tried to laugh but it came out strangled. "That's not where I'm hurting, Annie." He rolled his hips from side to side against Annie's widespread thighs, and Annie felt the clear delineation of the ridge pressing against her with an urgency that matched her own.

"Oh," she said.

Clay chuckled. "'Oh' about says it, darling." Then he chucked her under the chin.

"I've shocked you, haven't I?" she asked, belatedly shy.

Shocked would be the understatement of the year, Clay decided. *Who knew when I woke up this morning, a cold, dreary day in Princeton, that my evening would end in such a blaze of unexpected manna from heaven? But wait a minute. I don't like that look of second thoughts creeping onto Annie's face.* "Don't go shy on me now, Annie."

"I've never behaved this way before . . . so forward and uninhibited," she confessed, hiding her face in her hands.

"Your eagerness excites me. Tremendously. Don't you dare stop now," he said in a suffocated whisper, prying her fingers away. "I have plans for you that require a major dose of forwardness and un-inhibition."

"You do?"

Was that hope in her voice? "Absolutely. Are you afraid?"

"No. Are you?"

He laughed outright. God, how he loved her openness.

"Listen, Annie . . . stop, you witch . . . I can't think when you do that." She was leaning forward, her hair a thick swath curtaining his face, as she still straddled him. Back and forth, she was brushing her breasts across his chest hairs."

"That's the point, isn't it? Not to think?"

He leaned up and gave her a quick kiss. "You don't act like any virgin I've ever known." *Not that I've known very many . . . or any, for that matter, that I can recall.*

"Just because I didn't do *that*, doesn't mean I didn't do anything," she said, meanwhile kissing a little line from one end of his jaw to the other.

Clay fought against the roil of jealousy that ripped through him at the thought of any other man touching his Annie *in any way*. Had it been the milkman, or someone else? How many someone elses? "Annie, you're driving me mad. Be still for one moment. Please."

Surprisingly, she did as he asked. Of course, when she stilled, she also sat upright, square on his already overeager, over-engorged erection. He closed his eyes for one second, to keep them from bulging clear out of his head. Finally, when he managed to speak above a squeak, he said, "We're not going to make love tonight, Annie."

She stiffened at once, and her face went beet red. "You don't want me?"

"Of course, I want you, but I refuse to make love with you on an uncomfortable sofa . . . out in the open . . . with a houseful of people . . . no matter what you say about sleeping patterns or rules for . . . uh, courting."

She pondered his words, then seemed to accept their logic. "So, we're not going to make love *tonight?* Will we ever?"

"Oh, for sure, darling. For sure."

She smiled widely at that.

"And there's another thing, Annie-love. We have to talk about this thing that's happening with us."

"It is . . . strange."

"Strange, overpowering, confusing. I have an idea, Annie. Let's go out tomorrow night. Slow down this runaway train. See where this relationship is going."

"I like the sound of that."

He took a breast in each hand then and admired the contrast of the firm, white mounds against his darker skin. "I love your breasts. I love the way they aren't big, but appear to be so because of your thin frame." He stretched his head forward to savor one of them with his mouth.

She made a keening sound low in her throat, halfway between a purr and a cry for mercy. "I thought we weren't going to make love," she gasped out.

"True. We're not going to make love. But we can make out. A little."

"Oh, goody," she cooed. Before he knew what she was about, Annie slid a hand between them and caressed him. "Does this count as making love or making out?"

He about shot off the couch. And all he could think was, *Who the hell cares?* "Whoa, whoa, whoa, Annie." Very carefully, he dislodged her grasp and placed both her hands at her sides and held them there. "You've been running the show for much too long in your family. It's time for you to sit back and let someone else take over."

Her chin went up, balking.

"All right?"

After a long pause of hesitation, she nodded.

He proceeded then to unbutton her jeans.

Her eyebrows shot up in surprise, but she didn't protest.

"Lift up a little, honey, and lean forward," he advised. When she did, he slid a hand inside the waistband of her panties, down between her legs. The warm, wetness he met there caused him to sigh with pleasure. "Oh, Annie-love, you feel so good."

"Claaay," she cried out, unsure whether she wanted him to touch her there.

Before she had a chance to think further, he inserted a long middle finger inside her tightness and rested a pulsing thumb against the swollen bud. "Now, Annie," he encouraged her with a guttural hoarseness, "you ride . . . you set the pace."

"I . . . I don't think I can," she whimpered.

"Yes, you can, darling." And she did. With each forward thrust, she brushed the ridge of his erection. They were separated by denim material but the sensation was still intense. With each withdrawal, that part of his body yearned for her next stroke. It didn't last long. Probably only minutes. But when Annie began to spasm around his finger and melt onto him, he held her fast by the hips, leaned forward to kiss her with a devouring hunger, and bucked upward . . . once, twice, three times.

"Annie-love," he whispered into her hair a short time later. She was nestled at his side, both of them stretched out full-length on the sofa.

"Hmmm?" She was half-asleep and sated.

Clay couldn't have been prouder if he'd pulled off a million dollar investment deal. You'd think he was personally responsible for having made the world move. Well, he had, actually. For both of them.

"Clay?" she prodded.

"I'm think I'm falling in love with you," he disclosed. He hadn't intended to tell her . . . not yet. But his senses were on overload, brimming with so much joy. He couldn't contain it all.

"I already know I'm in love with you," she admitted. "I think I fell the minute I saw you storming across that vacant lot looking like Scrooge himself."

He poked her playfully in the ribs at that insult, but inside he felt such a triumphant sense of elation. *Annie loves me. Annie loves me. Annie loves me.* It was all so new and strange and confusing. Not what he'd come to Memphis to find. It would pose all kinds of problems in his life. But what a wonderful, wonderful thing! *Annie loves me.*

Annie worried her bottom lip with her teeth then. Obviously, she had something on her mind. Finally, she blurted out, "When will you know for sure?"

Clay chuckled and said, "Maybe after we check out the hayloft."

The best-laid plans of foolish men...

I love her.

It was Clay's first thought when he awakened the next morning to bright sunlight warming the cozy bedroom. You'd think it was springtime, instead of four days before Christmas. But then, Clay recalled, he was in Tennessee . . . almost the deep South.

With an open-mouthed yawn, he stretched widely, becoming immediately aware of the ache in his ankle and at the back of his head. He glanced to the side, saw the bedside clock, and jolted upright, causing the dull pain to intensify. *Ten o'clock!* He hadn't slept beyond six a.m. in the past twenty years.

Oh, well! First, he would take a shower. Afterward, he had at least a dozen calls to make, first to check with his office in New York, then to set the hotel sale in motion here in Memphis.

But there was only one thought that kept ringing through his head. *I love Annie.* Clay was not a whimsical person. If anyone had told him a few days ago that he would believe in love at first sight or romantic destiny, he would have scoffed, vehemently. He didn't know how it had happened or why, though he suspected, illogically, that it involved that dingbat bellhop and God's big toe and Elvis's spirit. He'd been fated to come to Memphis. Not to sell the blasted hotel, though he would do that as soon as possible, but to find Annie. *Amazing!*

It would take some doing to get Annie moved to Princeton. Probably, they'd have to wait till after the holidays. Oh, he knew it would be hard for her to leave the farm, but she had Chet and her brothers here to take over for her. And her Aunt Liza would care for the boys. Hell, he'd hire a live-in housekeeper to help Aunt Liza if necessary. Or the whole gang could come live with him, though he couldn't imagine that ever happening. It would be like the Clampetts moving to Princeton. All he knew was that it was time someone took care of Annie, and Clay thanked God it was going to be him.

Would they get married?

Of course. There was no way her family would allow her to live with a man without a wedding. And Annie would want that, too, Clay was sure.

How did he feel about marriage? Hmmm. A few days ago, he would have balked. But now . . . Clay smiled. Now, the idea of marrying Annie seemed ordained. Perfect.

So, everything was all set. He and Annie would go out tonight on a date. He would propose. She would accept. They'd make plans for the wedding and then move to Princeton. And a honeymoon . . . they'd fit a honeymoon in there, too. Perfect.

The only problem was that Clay kept hearing the oddest thing. Somewhere in the house, a radio was playing that old Elvis song, "Blue

Suede Shoes," but every time Elvis would belt out a stanza that was supposed to end in a warning not to step on "my blue suede shoes," Clay kept hearing, " . . . don't you step on *God's big toe.*"

If Clay was a superstitious man, he'd consider it a premonition.

He was getting love advice from Grandma Moses...

"You've got to be kidding!"

Clay had showered and shaved with a disposable razor he'd found in the bathroom. Then he'd unhesitatingly entered Chet's room where he borrowed a clean set of clothes, including a pair of new underwear straight from the package. This family owed him that, at least. Okay, he owed them a lot, too, he was beginning to realize . . . like a new life.

But now, Aunt Liza had forced him into a chair at the kitchen table where she'd placed in front of him a half dozen platters heaped with bacon and sausage, hot cakes drizzling butter and maple syrup, scrambled eggs and leftover biscuits from last night (also drizzling butter), slices of scrapple (which he'd heard contained pork unmentionables, like noses and things), black pudding (which Aunt Liza told him without blinking was blood sausage), coffee, orange juice, and a glass of cold milk with a header of pure cream.

"All I ever have for breakfast is coffee, juice and an English muffin, or toast," he demurred.

"Well, you ain't in New Jersey now, boy. So eat up. I got some oatmeal cookin' on the stove, too, to warm up your innards."

He groaned. "If I eat all this, I won't be able to move."

"You ain't goin' anywhere anyhow, sonny. You're stuck here on the farm with a gimp leg, in case you hadn't noticed."

"But I have work to do . . . calls to make—"

She slapped a couple of pig nose slabs on his plate and glared at him till he finally gave in. He pushed the pig nose slabs to the side, though, and gave himself modest helpings of eggs and biscuits, one sausage link, two slices of bacon, and one hot cake, but before he knew it his plate was overflowing.

Despite all his protests, the food was mouth-wateringly delicious, and he told Aunt Liza so. She smiled graciously at the compliment and sat down at the table with him, sipping at a cup of coffee.

"When did everyone leave for Memphis?" he asked as he ate . . . and ate . . . and ate.

"'Bout nine," Aunt Liza said, nibbling on a buttered biscuit, slathered with strawberry jam, while she continued to drink her coffee. "They wanted to get an early start today . . . hopin' the Christmas shoppers and tourists will be out early."

Clay nodded. "Why didn't they leave Jason here with you?"

Aunt Liza's shoulders slumped, and her parchment cheeks pinkened. "I can't be on my feet too long. Gotta take lots of naps. And sometimes I don't hear the baby when he cries."

Clay wished he hadn't asked when he saw the shame on her wrinkled face. He decided silence was a better route to take . . . in other words, shut his big mouth. So, he tentatively tasted a piece of the black pudding, which was surprisingly palatable. It didn't taste at all like blood . . . not that he knew what blood tasted like.

"So when you gonna make an honest woman of our Annie?" Aunt Liza asked unexpectedly.

His milk went down the wrong pipe as he sputtered. He probably had a cream mustache, to boot. "I haven't done anything to make Annie dishonest," he asserted, swiping at his mouth with a napkin.

Aunt Liza gave him a sidelong glance of skepticism. "That whisker burn she was sportin' on her cheeks this mornin' didn't come from a close shave, honey. Besides, Roy and Jerry Lee was sayin' somethin' 'bout 'pink and flustery' and 'guilty as sin.' Don't suppose you know what they was talkin' about?"

Clay hated the fact that his face was heating up, but he wasn't about to cower under the old buzzard's insinuations. He raised his chin obstinately and refused to rise to her bait.

"We got one loose chick hatched on this place and I don't want no more," Aunt Liza went on. "Randy roosters and footloose hens are runnin' rampant these days."

Clay didn't have the faintest idea what she was talking about. Roosters and hens and chicks?

"Now I don't countenance loose behavior none, but you best be keepin' these," she said, pulling a small box out of her apron pocket and shoving it his way, "just in case the devil sits on your shoulder sometime soon."

"Wh-what?" Clay stammered as he realized that Aunt Liza had handed him a box of condoms. *My God! A woman old enough to be my grandmother is giving me condoms.* "Where did you get these?"

"The supermarket."

"You . . . you went into a supermarket and bought condoms?"

"Yep. Durn tootin', I did. 'Bout caused ol' Charlie Good, the manager, to swallow his false teeth."

"You bought condoms *for me?* But . . . but I just got here yesterday." Clay's head was reeling with confusion.

"Don't be an idjit, boy. 'Tweren't you I bought those suckers for." Aunt Liza took another sip of coffee, ignoring the fact that he was waiting, slack-jawed, for her next bombshell. "Chet learned his lesson good, I reckon, with that little chick of his. But I was figurin' on havin' a talk with Hank. That boy's headed on the road to ruination sure as God made Jezebels and hot-blooded roosters."

Hank? She bought the condoms for Hank? That makes sense. I guess. Whew!

"This whole generation's goin' to hell in a handbasket, if you ask me." Aunt Liza clucked a tsk-ing sound, piercing him with a stare that included him in the wild bunch. "I blame it all on the tongue business."

The tongue business? Don't ask. Don't ask. "What tongue business?"

"Tongue kissin'. What tongue business didja think I was gabbin' about?" she answered tartly, as if he should have known better. "When courtin' couples start tongue kissin', the trouble begins. Next thing ya know they're buyin' Pampers by the gross." She narrowed her eyes at Clay, and he just knew Aunt Liza was going to ask him if he'd been giving Annie tongue. Before she could speak, he put up a halting hand. Time to put some brakes on this outrageous conversation.

"Aunt Liza," Clay said in the calmest voice he could muster without breaking out in laughter, "Annie and I have not had sex." *Yet.* "But even if we had, whatever happened or didn't happen or is about to happen is between me and Annie."

"Well, that may very well be, Mr. Hoity-Toity City Feller, but if there's a weddin' to be planned, I gotta commence makin' a menu, and preparin' food. Everyone in the whole county will wanna come to Annie Fallon's weddin', that's for sure. I don't wanna be goin' to all that trouble for a bride with a belly what looks like she swallowed a watermelon seed nine months past."

I'm going insane. I just discovered I'm falling in love, and already she has me making babies and walking down the aisle, in that order. And, Good Lord, does she think we would get married in a farmhouse? With pigs' noses and cows' blood and other equally distasteful stuff on the wedding menu?

Now that was unkind. She's only being concerned. You really are being hoity-toity, if that means the same as poker-up-your butt snobbish. C'mon, Jessup, stop acting like you're in stodgy, hoity-toity Princeton.

"Aunt Liza, if and when Annie and I decide to marry, you'll be the first to know."

"Oh, I know, all right," she said, leveling him with a scrutiny that saw right through his facade. "I knew the minute Annie brung you through that door yesterday. I knew when the radio kept bopping on and off all day with Elvis music that his spirit has come into the house. I knew when you gawked at Annie all durin' dinner last night and couldn't keep the love out of your eyes. I knew—"

"Enough!" he said with a laugh of surrender. "Pass me the pigs' noses."

Chapter Five

The punishment for tongue is...

Clay was waiting on the front porch when Annie got home at five.

She felt the now familiar feverish heat envelop her the minute he came into view. It was the strangest, most wonderful, scariest feeling in the world to drive up in the pickup and see this man she'd come to love in such a short time, just standing there waiting for her to come home.

Leaning against a porch post, he was dressed in his neatly pressed suit, the sides of his jacket pulled back over his slim hips by hands which were tucked into the pockets of his slacks. One crutch was propped beside him. It was a casual pose, but Annie could see he was as nervous and excited as she was.

"Hi," she said breathlessly, coming up the steps.

"Hi," he said back, his eyes crinkling with amusement as they skimmed over her, from bouffant hair to Blessed Mary robe.

She stopped midway up the steps, an attack of timidity overcoming her. All day she'd been thinking about him, the wicked things he'd done to her last night, how he'd made her feel. Now, all the thoughts she'd wanted to share with him stuck in her throat. What if he'd changed his mind? What if his heart wasn't racing as madly as hers? What if he didn't really want to take her out on a date tonight? What if he didn't love her?

Clay uncoiled himself from his leaning position and stepped forward, slowly. One hand snaked out to grasp her by the nape and draw her closer. "I missed you," he husked out.

"Oh, God, I missed you too. But I look awful," she said, waggling her fingers in a flustery fashion to indicate her caricature appearance. *Flustery? I'm probably pink, too. Roy and Jerry Lee were right. Flustery and pink.*

Clay chuckled. "Just shows how far gone I am. You're beginning to look good, even as a sixties Madonna." He dragged her close and lowered his head toward hers. Annie watched, mesmerized, as his eyelids fluttered closed and his lips parted.

Then she forgot everything, too engrossed in the kiss that seared her already feverish body to her very soul. When he slipped his tongue inside her mouth, she felt his heat, and knew the fever had overtaken him, as well.

She moaned against his open mouth.

He moaned back.

A sharp rapping noise jarred them both from their kiss, ending it far too soon. It was Aunt Liza, using her wooden spoon to knock a warning on the kitchen window that looked out over the porch. "There better not be any tongue business goin' on," Aunt Liza called out. "Remember what I told you, young man."

Annie leaned back, still in the circle of Clay's arms, and peered questioningly up at him.

He laughed. "You don't want to know."

"Hey, Clay," Chet greeted him. Still dressed in his Elvis/St. Joseph gear and high, duck tail hairdo, Chet had just come from the pickup truck where he must have been gathering the baby's paraphernalia, which was looped over his one shoulder. The baby, held in the other arm at his other shoulder, was wide-awake and gurgling happily, swatting at Chet's nose with a rattle. Chet must have heard Aunt Liza because he waggled his eyebrows with commiseration and commented, "Aunt Liza gave you the tongue lecture, right?"

"Oh, no!" Annie groaned, putting her face in her hands.

"We made eight hundred dollars today," Johnny informed him cheerily as he skipped up the steps, Elvis hair bouncing up and down. His sheepskin shepherd outfit was in sharp contrast to his duct-taped sneakers. "Annie says I can get a new pair of athletic shoes for Christmas if we keep going at this clip. And, see, Annie. I didn't say one single word about `pink and flustery,' just like you warned."

"Where do you think you're going?" Annie asked Johnny. "There's milking to be done."

"I know, I know. Don't get your dander up. I have to go to the bathroom first. They can start without me," he whined, pointing at his brothers.

Roy, Hank and Jerry Lee, still dolled up as Elvis Wise Men, were unloading the donkey and two sheep from the animal van, alternately smirking toward him and Annie and trying to get the stubborn donkey to move. At one point, Roy and Jerry Lee were shoving the donkey's butt while Roy pulled on a lead rope. The only thing they accomplished was a load of donkey manure barely missing their feet.

"I swear, Annie, I'm butchering this donkey come Christmas," Roy vowed.

Clay tasted bile rising in his throat. They wouldn't really eat donkey, would they? Hell, they ate beef blood and pigs' noses. Why not donkey? "Hurry and shower so we can go out," he whispered to Annie. "I have big plans for tonight."

"Big plans? Oh, my! I certainly hope so."

"Before you shower, we better go out to the barn and breed Mirabelle. She's not gonna be in heat much longer. I don't think we wanna wait another twenty-one days for her to go in heat again." Clay hadn't realized that Chet still stood on the porch, behind them. "Here," Chet added, handing the baby to Clay, "take him in the house for me. We'll be back in a half hour or so."

"What? Who? Me?" Clay said, staring at the wide-eyed baby who gaped at him as if his father had just delivered him to King Kong. Clay was holding the kid gingerly with hands under both his tiny armpits. Just when Clay thought the baby was going to let loose with a wail of outrage, Jason gave him a slobbery smile and belted him on the forehead with a rattle.

Clay could swear he heard Aunt Liza giggling on the other side of the kitchen window. She probably considered it just payment for tongue.

Cow sex wasn't for the weak of heart ... or stomach ...

A half hour later, Annie hadn't returned to the house. Aunt Liza had changed baby Jason after Clay had performed the amazing feat of feeding him a bottle. The kid, who was really quite precious, was now cooing contentedly from his infant seat in the kitchen where he was pulverizing a piece of melba toast.

Clay decided to check out this cow breeding business.

What he saw when he entered the huge barn stunned him. First of all, there was the overpowering smell. Cow manure, the hot earthy scent of animal flesh, and fresh milk. A cow belched near him and he almost jumped out of his wingtips. The sweet reek of the cow's breath that drifted toward him on the wake of the cow burp was not unpleasant, but strange. Very strange.

There was a center aisle with about sixty black and white cows lined up in stalls on both sides. Jerry Lee was washing down cow udders and stimulating teats, while Roy was hooking the teats up to automated milking contraptions, six cows at a time.

Hank was shoveling feed in the troughs for the big cows, which must weigh about fifteen-hundred pounds, at the same time ministering to the sixty or so young stock at the far end of the barn. The whole time he was addressing the cows by name. Florence. Sweet Caroline. Aggie. Winona. Rosie Posie. Lucille. Pamela Lee. On and on, he chatted with the cows. How he ever remembered all the names, Clay didn't know.

Johnny was sitting off to the side bottle feeding a half dozen baby calves. "Hey, Clay, wanna help me?" he asked.

"Uh . . . I don't think I'm dressed for that," he declined. Besides, he wanted to see what Annie was doing at the other end of the barn. She and Chet were in a separate, larger stall with one humongous cow about the size of a minivan. That must be the breeding section.

"Where's the bull?" he inquired casually, as if he strolled through barns every day to view cow sex.

Chet and Annie jerked to attention. Apparently they hadn't heard him come up behind them. Well, no wonder. With all these cows mooing, he could barely hear anything himself.

"We don't have any bulls," Annie answered. "We butcher or sell off all the male stock."

"Why?"

"Bulls are too darn ornery, that's why," Chet answered. "They're not worth the trouble, believe me."

"But . . . but how do you breed the cows then?"

"Artificial insemination," Chet informed him. "This is the twenty-first century, man."

It was only then that he noticed Chet was holding the cow still, even though it was tied by a loose rope to the front of the stall. Annie, on the other hand, stood there with a big brown apron covering her Virgin Mary gown. On one arm, she wore a plastic glove that reached all the way to the shoulder. In the other hand, she held a huge syringe-type affair, more like a twenty-inch caulking gun.

My Lord!

"You better step back," Chet warned him.

Clay's eyes bugged and his mouth dropped open before he spun on his heels and rushed outside . . . where he proceeded to hurl the contents of his stomach which Aunt Liza had taken great pains to stuff all day long.

I wonder where this ranks in the God's Big Toe category?

It's now or never...

Clay had almost botched things, bigtime.

At first, it had seemed as if their blooming relationship had been slam-dunked back to step one, or zero, with his disastrous reaction to that scene in the barn. He still shivered with distaste at what he'd seen, but he was doing his shivering internally. The sooner he could erase that picture from his mind, the better. In time—maybe ten or twenty years—he would, no doubt, forget it totally.

Annie had appeared crushed when she'd followed him out of the barn. He could understand that. Farm work, in all its crude aspects, was what Annie did for a living—her identity. It had been obvious that Annie thought he was repulsed by her. *Not her, what she'd been doing.* But Clay hadn't dared say that. Instead, he'd lied, "My stomach has been upset all day. It must be the after-effects of those pain killers, or something I ate."

She'd stared at him dubiously. "Maybe it's not such a good idea for us to go out on a date. Things have been happening too fast. We haven't stopped to consider our differences. It's probably a good idea for us to slow down and count to ten—"

Reconsider? Count to ten? No way! We're not even counting to two. Oh, God! She's going to dump us. He'd backpedaled then and convinced her to give him another chance. At what, he wasn't sure. He only knew he loved her, cow breeding or no cow breeding. And he didn't want to blow the best thing that had ever happened to him.

Now, strolling down Memphis's famous Beale Street, he was getting yet another view of his Annie. This one he liked a whole lot better than all the rest. So far, he'd had the Priscilla Virgin Mary, the jeans and flannel farm girl (He was still waiting for the Daisy Mae outfit, darn it!) and the cow breeder to the bovine stars. Now, Annie wore a calf-length floral print skirt of some crinkled gauze material over a satin lining. It was robin egg blue with gold flowers. On top was a long-sleeved, matching blue sweater of softest cashmere that reached her hips and was belted at the waist. The gold flowers of the skirt were picked up in embroidery around the sweater's neckline. It was probably a Thrift Shop purchase, knowing Annie, who spent nothing on herself. On her legs she wore sheer stocking and black high heels that did amazing things to her already amazing legs. Her lustrous brown hair was pulled off her face by gold clips and hung in disarray to her shoulders. She'd even used some makeup—a little blush, mascara, and lip gloss, as far as he could tell. She looked smart and sexy. Sort of like a young Julia Roberts, but better, to his mind, as he'd thought before. No wonder he'd fallen head over heels in love with her.

Clay couldn't stop looking at her.

And she couldn't stop looking at him.

He smiled at her.

She smiled back.

He was using one crutch to keep his full weight off his sprained ankle, which was almost better today. With his free hand, Clay twined Annie's fingers with his.

She swung their clasped hands.

Clay couldn't understand how he got so much pleasure from just holding hands with a woman and hobbling slowly down the street. Annie had been giving him a running commentary on the history of Memphis.

"Are you sure you don't want to eat yet?" she inquired. "It's almost eight o'clock."

He shook his head. They'd already passed up hot tamales and greasy burgers at the Blues City Cafe, where Tom Cruise had filmed a scene for the movie, "The Firm," as well as ribs, catfish and world famous fried dill pickles, the specialties at B.B. King's Club.

"How about this?" Annie had stopped in front of Lansky Brothers/Center for Southern Folklore. "This museum is dedicated to preserving the legends and folklore of the entire south, but especially Memphis. They have an excellent photography collection here."

"My mother was a photographer," Clay revealed. *Now, why did I mention that? I never talk about my mother.*

"Really? Did she use her maiden name or her married name?" Annie was already tugging him by the hand to enter the small museum where a plaque informed him it was the site of the former Lansky Brothers Clothing Store where Elvis, B.B. King, Jerry Lee Lewis, Carl Perkins and others had purchased their clothes.

Well, that impresses the hell out of me. I'd want to buy my boxers in the same store as Elvis, for sure.

But Clay knew he was dwelling on irrelevant garbage to avoid thinking about Annie's question. Finally, he answered, "Her maiden name. Clare Gannett."

"Clare Gannett? Clare Gannett? Why, she's famous, Clay."

"She is . . . was . . . not!" he said with consternation.

"Well, not Annie Liebowitz famous, but she has a fame of sorts here in Memphis"

It doesn't take much to be famous in Memphis. Just be a store that sold Elvis a pair of boxers. Or the barber who gave him a haircut. Or the playground where he scraped his shin.

"Annie, my mother was not a famous photographer. For one thing, she died when she was only twenty-eight . . . whoa . . . wait a minute . . . what are you doing?" Annie paid for two tickets, and was pulling him determinedly past the exhibits into another room.

"See," she said, pointing to one wall where there were a series of photos of Elvis Presley...an older Elvis. In fact, going by the dates under the frames, they must have been taken a few years before his mother had died in 1979; after all, Elvis had left the world in 1977. They were casual shots . . . leaning against a car, strumming a guitar, standing in front of The Blue Suede Suites. A framed document explained that Clare Gannett, despite her youth, had been one of Memphis's premier photographers, documenting on film many of the city's early music performers during the mid to late seventies . . . not just Elvis, but many rock and blues personalities who later went on to fame.

Oh, great! My mother knew Elvis. First, I find out my father owned a hokey hotel named after one of Elvis's songs. Now, I find out my mother must have known the king. What next?

"Legend says that Elvis loved Clare Gannett—"

Clay put his face in his hands. He didn't want to hear this.

"—but she fell in love with some Yankee who came to Memphis on a business trip one day. They say the Yankee bought the hotel and next-door property where her studio was located as a wedding present for her. The studio later burned down, and Clare Gannett died in the fire. The hotel owner, your father, refused to erect anything else on that site. Isn't that romantic?"

"Annie, that is nothing but bullshit propaganda, a silly yarn spun for gullible tourists."

"Maybe. But legend says Elvis was heartbroken over losing Clare Gannett. He died the same year she got married. I know, I know, there are a lot of legends and rumors in there, but still..."

Clay turned angrily and stomped as fast as he could on one crutch out of the building. He was breathing heavily, in and out, trying to control his rage.

"Clay, what's wrong?" Annie asked softly. She came up close to him and put a hand on his suit sleeve.

He waited several seconds before speaking, not wanting to take out his ill-feelings on Annie. "Annie, my mother abandoned me and my father when I was only one year old. So, your telling me she had a relationship with that hip-swiveling jerk doesn't sit too well with me, even if it was before her marriage to my father."

"I'm sorry, Clay. But maybe you're wrong about her. The legend never said that she loved Elvis. In fact, she supposedly broke Elvis's heart when she married your father. Maybe—"

He leaned down to kiss her softly, the best way he could think of to halt her words. "It was a long time ago. It doesn't matter anymore."

She gazed at him with tears in her eyes. *Tears, for God's sake!* Not for a moment did she buy his unconcern.

"Hey, let's go in this place," Clay suggested cheerily, coming to a standstill in front of *Forever Blue,* a small jazz club. He desperately sought a change of mood. "It doesn't seem as crowded as some of the other joints."

He guided her in front of him into the club and an empty table where they ordered drinks and a mushroom and sundried tomato pizza. A short time later, with the backdrop of a piano player filling the room with classic jazz tunes, Clay moved his chair close to Annie and fiddled with the edges of her hair . . . nervous as a teenager on his first date.

"Annie-love," he whispered, kissing the curve of her neck. She smelled of some light floral fragrance . . . lilies of the valley, maybe. As always, there was this delicious heat ricocheting between them.

"Hmmm?" she purred, arching her neck to give him greater access.

"I don't want to go back to the farm . . . yet."

"Me neither," she breathed, turning to stare directly into his eyes.

"Will you come back to my hotel room with me?"

Annie continued to stare into his eyes, unwavering. She had to know what he was asking. Finally, she nodded, leaning closer to place her lips against his, softly. "I have to go back to the farm tonight, though. There's the four a.m. milking before we return to Memphis for the Nativity Scene."

He stiffened at the thought of the woman he loved demeaning herself in that ridiculous sideshow. "Annie, stay home at the farm tomorrow. Give up the Nativity Scene venture. Let me help you . . . and your family . . . financially."

She immediately bristled. "No! The Fallon Family doesn't accept charity."

He should have known she'd balk. But, dammit, how was she going to reconcile accepting his money after they were married? "Whatever you say, sweetheart. It was only a suggestion," he conceded, *for now.*

She softened at his half-hearted apology. "I want to be with you, Clay," she whispered.

"Not half as much as I want to be with you."

Clay barely noticed the piano player, the singing crowd, or the loud surroundings of the club. All he could think about was Annie and the fact they were going to be together tonight. It appeared as if it would turn out all right, after all. No more celestial big toes.

He hoped.

He rousted her about, all right, and she rousted him, too...

Annie was nervous, but exhilarated, as they entered the foyer of The Blue Suede Suites.

It was only ten o'clock and the hotel lobby still buzzed with activity, its guests coming in for the evening, or just going out, in some cases. As myriad as Memphis itself, the guests ranged from sedately dressed businessmen to a group of Amazing Soaring Elvi. But mostly there were tourists come to view the spectacle that was Memphis, the adopted home of Elvis . . . like those two middle-aged women over there in neon pink "Elvis Lives" sweatshirts who were eyeing Clay as if they thought he might be someone famous.

"They think I'm George," Clay informed her dryly, noticing her line of vision.

"George who?"

Clay shrugged. "Damned if I know. Straight, or Strayed, or something like that."

Annie burst out in laughter. "George Strait?"

"Yes. That's the one."

Annie hugged the big dolt. "How could anyone in the modern world not know George Strait? Clay, you are too, too precious."

He grinned at her calling him precious, then took her hand and led her around the massive Christmas tree in the center of the lobby. It was decorated with sparkling lights and priceless rock star memorabilia left by the various musicians who'd stayed in this hotel over the years. A gold-plated guitar pick from Chet Atkins. Guitar strings tied into a bow, from Hank Williams. A silver star that had once adorned the dressing room of Eddie Arnold. Pearl earrings from Tammy Wynette.

"Have you ever seen such a gaudy tree in all your life?"

"Clay, you need a major attitude adjustment."

"And you're the one to give it to me, aren't you, Annie-love," he said, flicking her chin playfully. "Come on. I need to pick up something at the desk."

David and Marion Bloom, the long-time managers, nodded at Clay as he approached, and then at Annie, too. The refined couple, who resembled David Niven and Ingrid Bergman, right down to the thin mustache and the neatly coiled French twist hairdo, respectively, were probably surprised to see Annie with their boss, but they didn't betray their reactions by so much as a lifted eyebrow.

"Did an express mail package come for me today?" Clay asked.

"Yes, sir," David Bloom said, drawing a cardboard mailer out of a drawer behind the desk.

"And I have all those tax statements you asked me to gather together when you called this afternoon," Marion Bloom added.

Clay took the mailer, but waved aside the stack of papers. "I'll examine those tomorrow."

Annie could see that the Blooms looked rather pale, their faces pinched with worry. Heck, everyone at the hotel was alarmed, from what Annie had heard when in Memphis earlier today. The possibility of imminent unemployment once the hotel closed had them all walking on tenterhooks, especially with the holidays looming. Annie would have liked to tell them that Clay would never close the hotel now that he knew what a landmark it was to Memphis, not to mention the connection with his mother. But it wasn't her place to speak on his behalf.

"We'll meet tomorrow at one with the accountant, right?" Clay asked the couple. When they nodded solemnly, he concluded, "Good Night, then," and led Annie toward the elevators.

Once the doors swished shut, Annie leaned her head on Clay's shoulder and sighed. But he set her away from him and stepped to the other side of the elevator, staring at her with a rueful grimace. "If I touch you now, sweetheart, we'll be having sex on the elevator floor."

She smiled.

"You little witch. You'd like that, wouldn't you?" Clay observed with a chuckle.

Soon he was inserting the key into the lock of his hotel room. Once they entered, Clay flicked on the light switch, and Annie was assaulted with a dozen different sounds, sights and smells. A carousel—*A carousel, for heaven's sake!*—was turning in one corner of the massive suite, churning out calliope music. A television in another corner clicked on automatically, playing a video of that old Elvis movie "Roustabout." A popcorn machine began popping and a candy cotton machine began spinning its weblike confection. Hot dogs sizzled on a counter grill, where candy apples were laid out for a late-night snack. And the bed . . . Holy Cow! . . . the bed was in the form of a Tunnel of Love cart with high sides, and what looked like a vibrating mechanism on the side to simulate a water rocking motion.

"Cla-ay!" she laughed.

"Did you ever see anything so absurd in all your life?" A delightful pink stained his cheeks.

"Actually, it's kind of . . . uh, charming."

"Please," he begged to differ. Then, tossing his crutch aside, he leaned back against the door and pulled her into his embrace. "At last," he whispered against her mouth.

When he kissed her, open-mouthed and clinging, Annie could taste his need for her. What a heart-filling ego booster to know she could affect this man so!

With clumsy haste, they pulled at each other's clothes.

"Slow down, honey," Clay urged raggedly, then immediately reversed himself. "No, hurry up, sweetheart."

"I can't wait, I can't wait, I can't wait . . . ," she cried.

Soon they were naked. He with nothing but a bandage wrapped around his one ankle, she with nothing but two gold barrettes which she quickly tossed aside.

She saw his arousal and felt her own arousal throb in counterpoint. Leaning forward, she pressed her lips to his chest, breathing in the clean, musky scent of his skin.

Clay gasped.

"You are so hot," she blurted out.

He grinned. "I know."

"Oh, you! I meant you throw off heat like . . . like an erotic bonfire."

Clay laughed. "So do you, Annie. So do you," he whispered, holding her face with the fingertips of both hands. He gazed at her with sheer adulation, which both humbled and exalted her. Tears filled her eyes at the admiration she saw in his wonderful blue eyes.

"I love you, Clayton Jessup. I don't know how it's possible to fall in love with someone so fast and so hard, but it's the truth. I love you."

"I feel as if I've been walking through life with a huge hole in my heart and now, suddenly, it's been filled. You make me complete, Annie. I know, that sounds so corny—"

"Shhh," she said, putting a forefinger against his lips. "It doesn't sound corny at all."

He led her to the bed then and they climbed over the ridiculously high side frames, laughing. It was an awkward exercise, with Clay's injury.

"At least there's no danger of us falling out of bed if you get too rambunctious," she teased.

In response, he swatted her on the behind, which was raised ignominiously in the air before she plopped down next to him.

Turning serious, Clay turned onto his back and adjusted her so she lay half over him. Then he took her hands, encouraging her to explore him.

And she did.

Oh, Lord, she did.

She told him things she'd never imagined were in the far reaches of her fantasies. She used words . . . wicked words, which drew a heated blush to her cheeks, and a chuckle of satisfaction from Clay.

Clay told her things, too, in a voice silky with sex. He spoke of erotic activities that made her tremble with trepidation. Or was it anticipation?

"I never expected that a man's hands could be so gentle and aggressive, at the same time," she confessed.

"Who knew you'd be so passionate!" Clay said as he performed magic feats on the many surfaces of her body. "I love the soft sounds you make when I touch you here. And here. And here."

Clay nudged her knees apart and lay over her, weight braced on his elbows. He teased her nipples with his fingers and lips and teeth and tongue—plucking, sucking, fluttering and nipping—till Annie ached for more. It was hard to believe that the staid businessman could be such an inventive lover.

Finally, finally, finally, he penetrated her, and there was no pain, just a stretching fullness. Clay went still, his body taut with tension as he watched her from extended arms

"I love you, Annie," he whispered.

Her inner folds shifted around him in response, allowing him to grow even more, filling her even more.

"I love you, too, Clay. With all my heart."

Only then did he begin to move. Long strokes that seemed to draw her very soul from her body. Then he surged back in again. Over and over, he took her breath away, then gave her new life.

She drew her knees up to give him greater access.

His heart thundered against her breast.

"Come for me, Annie," he gritted out painfully. "Let it happen, love."

But Annie fought her climax till she saw Clay rear his head back, veins taut in his neck, and let loose with a raw animal sound of pure male release as he plunged deep into her depths. Only then did Annie allow herself to spasm around him in progressively stronger reflexes till she, too, cried out with the pure pleasure-pain.

Annie wept then. Not from physical soreness, or emotional distress. It was the beauty and rightness of what they shared that drew her tears. There was a dampness in Clay's eyes, too.

After that, they made love again. A slow, serious exploration of each other's bodies, their likes and dislikes.

Then they made love a third time . . . a joyous, rib-tickling affair, involving mattress wave machines and carousels and sinfully sweet cotton candy.

Chapter Six

The perfect ending to a perfect night...

It was two o'clock in the morning, and she and Clay were sitting on the floor watching "Roustabout." She wore only Clay's dress shirt, he wore only a pair of boxers. She'd never enjoyed a movie more.

They were eating candy apples and chili dogs. He'd balked at the food choice, at first, but Annie noticed that he'd then scarfed down two of both in record time, washed down with a Coke. "We have to go back to the farm soon," she said regretfully. "We don't want to arrive when everyone is already waking up for the day. Talk about 'pink and flustery!' I'd be more like red and catatonic . . . with mortification."

"You aren't having second thoughts, are you?" Clay stood up and was taking their empty plates and glasses over to the kitchenette counter. He stopped and stared at her with concern.

"No, sweetheart, I'm not ashamed of anything we've done together. I just don't want to broadcast it to the world yet."

"Good," he said. "Because I have something for you." Clay went over to the hallway where he'd placed the express mailer that Mr. Bloom had handed to him earlier. Pulling the string zip, he took out a small box and handed it to Annie.

She raised her brows with uncertainty, then stood up and opened the small cardboard board. Inside, was a velvet box. Annie felt a roaring in her ears, and she began to weep, before she even opened the tiny latch to see an old-fashioned diamond in a gold setting, surrounded by diamond chips.

"It belonged to my grandmother. I called my office this morning and had my secretary take it out of the safety deposit box and mail it to me. If you don't like it, we can buy a new one, whatever you want." Clay was rambling on nervously while Annie continued to weep.

"It's beautiful," she sobbed.

"Will you marry me, love?"

"Of course, I'll marry you," she said and continued to sob.

"Here, let me put it on for you," Clay urged, a tearful thread in his voice, too.

It was dazzling. Not too big. Not too modern. Ideal.

"Oh, Clay, I love you so much."

"I love you, too. More than I ever thought possible."

They kissed to seal their betrothal.

Then they sealed their betrothal in another way.

Troubled waters, for sure, and no bridge in sight...

"How soon before we can get married, do you think?" Clay asked much later. "I've got to get back to my office sometime soon, and I hate the thought of leaving you behind."

"I don't know. Aunt Liza will want to have a big wedding, but we can do something small, for family only."

"Is that what you want?"

"I'm not sure. I always pictured myself walking down the aisle in a white gown . . . the works. But now . . . well, I want to be married to you as soon as possible."

"We'll have a big wedding, if that's what you always wanted, Annie-love. But we'll set a new time record for arranging a big wedding. Okay?"

She nodded, unable to stop staring at the beautiful ring on her finger.

"Will you be able to come back to Princeton with me for a while? Would that be too scandalous for Aunt Liza?"

Annie laughed. "Oh, I think we could convince her that your housekeeper is chaperon enough, but I couldn't stay for more than a week. It's too much to ask Chet and the others to take on my work for much more than that."

"But, honey, at some point they'll have to pick up your slack. When you move up north, they'll have no choice but to—"

The small choked sound Annie made caught Clay mid-sentence.

"Annie . . . Annie, what's wrong?"

Stricken, she could only stare at him. "You think I'll move to New Jersey, permanently?"

A frown creased Clay's forehead. "Of course. You didn't think I would be moving here, did you?"

"Yes," she wailed. "You didn't think I'd give up the farm, did you?"

"Yes."

They were both gaping at each other with incredulity.

"How could you think that you and I would marry and live in that farmhouse? It's too small for your family, as it is."

Annie shrugged. "I guess I wasn't thinking that far. At some point, Chet will probably marry Emmy Lou, once he gets his head together. And I would imagine they'll live at the farmhouse. But we could always build a house somewhere else on our land. There's plenty of acreage."

"Annie, I'm not a farmer."

"Well, I am," she stormed, then softened her voice, putting a hand up to cup Clay's rigid jaw, lovingly. "Clay, isn't there any way you could do your work from Memphis?"

"Annie, my business has been operated from the same Manhattan office by three generations of Jessups. My family home has been in Princeton for almost a hundred years."

"You didn't answer my question."

"I am *not* moving to Memphis, and that's final." He pleaded with her to understand, "That farm of yours is a money drain, pure and simple. This afternoon, rather yesterday afternoon, I read some of the farm magazines sitting around your house. You don't have to be a rocket scientist to know that eventually you'll have to sell off some land to developers or use hormones in your cattle feed. You're about twenty years behind the times, babe."

"How dare you . . . how dare you presume to tell me how to run my farm? And you know nothing about me, at all, if you think I would ever sell off even a shovelful of Fallon land."

"It's an unwise financial decision, Annie. Believe me, this is what I do for a living. This is my expertise."

"You can shove your expertise, Clay Jessup. And you can shove this, too," she said, taking off the ring and handing it back to him. The whole time tears were streaming down her face.

"Annie, don't. Oh, God, don't leave like this," he said, watching with horror as she snatched up her clothes and began to dress as quickly as possible. "Let's talk about this. You're not being rational." He began to dress, as well.

"You're not coming back to the farm with me."

"I don't want you driving alone in the middle of the night."

"I'm a big girl, Clay. I've been doing it for a long time."

Dressed now, she stared at him for a long moment. "Tell me one thing, Clay. Do you still intend to raze this hotel?"

"Of course. What would ever make you think otherwise?"

Annie tried, but couldn't stifle the sob that rose through her tight throat. "Call me crazy, but I thought you were developing a heart."

"You're being unfair."

"Life's unfair, Clay." She grabbed her shoulder bag and headed toward the door, anxious to be out of his sight now, before she broke down completely.

"I love you, Annie."

Her only response was to slam the door in his face.

Clay gazed at the closed door with abject misery.

How could I have made such a mess of things? How will I survive without Annie? What should I do now?

And somewhere, whether it was the television or inside his head, Clay couldn't tell for sure, Elvis gave him the answer, "I'm So Lonesome I Could Cry."

Truer words were never spoken.

And Clay was pretty sure this qualified as a God's Big Toe stumble.

And then the other shoe dropped...

Two days later, on Wednesday, a despondent Clay stared out his hotel room window as Annie and her brothers dismantled their live Nativity Scene for the day. Tomorrow was Christmas Eve; so, it would probably be their last day on the site.

Clay had no idea if he'd ever see Annie again after that.

Oh, he'd tried to reconcile their differences, but Annie wouldn't budge.

"Are you still selling the hotel?" she'd demanded to know yesterday when he'd confronted her in the hotel coffee shop. She and her family had managed to deflect all his phone calls before that. She'd even threatened to give up their live Nativity Scene yesterday, despite her family's need for money, if he didn't stop coming out and "bothering" her. "Well, answer me. Are you still selling the hotel?"

"Yes, but it has nothing to do with us, Annie. It's a business decision."

She'd made a harrumphing sound of disgust. "Would you move to Memphis?"

"Well, maybe we could live here part of the time . . . have homes in New Jersey and Tennessee." *See, I can compromise. Why can't you, Annie?* "Would you be willing to promise to never . . . uh . . . to never stick your arm up a cow's butt again?"

Annie had looked surprised at that request. Then she'd shaken her head sadly. "Clay, Clay, Clay. You just don't get it, do you? I've bred a hundred cows in my lifetime. I'll breed hundreds more before I die. If you think cow breeding is gross, you ought to see me butcher a pig. Or wring a chicken's neck, cut off its head, de-gut and de-feather it, all in time for dinner. Believe me, cow breeding is no big deal."

It is to me. And I refuse to picture Annie with a dead chicken, or cow. She's just kidding. She must be. "Don't you love me, Annie?" He'd hated the pathetic tone his voice had taken on then, but the question had needed to be asked.

"Yes, but I'm hoping I'll get over it."

No! his mind had screamed. *Don't get over it. You can't get over it. I won't. I can't.*

That had been the last conversation he'd had with the woman he loved and had lost, all in the space of a few lousy days in Memphis. Then today he'd discovered a card table in the lobby with the sign "Blue Suede Suites Employee Fund." Apparently, Annie and her family had donated two hundred dollars of their hard-earned money to start a fund for hotel employees who would soon be out of work, *due to him.* Annie had found a way, after all, to make him, albeit indirectly, the recipient of the Fallon Family Christmas Good Deed of the Year. And it didn't matter one damn bit to anyone that he'd dropped five hundred dollars in the box. Not that he'd told anyone.

A knock on the door jarred him from his daydream. It was the elderly bellhop. "Mr. and Mrs. Bloom said to tell you the lawyers'll be here any minute. Best you come down to the office to go over some last minute details for the sale."

The bellhop glared at him, then turned on his heels and stomped away, not even waiting for Clay to accompany him. Hell, the entire hotel staff, except for the Blooms, had put him on their freeze list. You'd think he was Simon Lagree. Or Scrooge.

Minutes later, Clay was in the manager's office, doing a last read-through of the legal documents. The attorneys hadn't arrived yet, and David had gone out front to register a guest.

"Mr. Jessup, I have some things that belongs to you . . . well, they belonged to your mother, but I guess that means they belong to you now."

"What?" Clay glanced up to see Marion lifting a cardboard box from a closet shelf.

"When the fire occurred at the photography studio next door, all those years ago, I was on duty. I managed to save a few scraps of things from the fire," she explained nervously.

"Why didn't you send them to my father?"

"I tried to give them to him when he came to Memphis to bury your mother, but he refused to take them . . . said he wanted nothing to remind him of her. It was the grief speaking, of course."

No, it wasn't the grief speaking. That's how my father regarded my mother his entire life.

Hesitantly he opened the box. On top was an eight-by-ten photograph, brown on the edges.

"It was their wedding picture," Mrs. Bloom informed him.

Clay felt as if he'd been kicked in the gut. His father—a much younger, carefree version than he'd ever witnessed—was dressed in a dark suit with a flower in the label, gazing with adoration at the woman standing at his side carrying a small bouquet of roses. Their arms were linked around each other's waists. She wore a stylish white suit with matching high heels, and she was staring at her new husband with pure, seemingly heartfelt love. They were standing on the steps in front of a church.

"How could two people who appear to have loved each other so much have fallen out of love so quickly?"

Marion gasped. "Whatever are you talking about? They never stopped loving each other."

Clay cut her with a sharp glower. "My mother abandoned me and my father."

"She never did so!" Marion snapped indignantly. "Clare came here to tie up some loose ends with her business, and to give her and your father some breathing room over their differences. But they never stopped loving each other."

He started to speak, but Marion put up a hand to halt his words. "You have to understand that there's something about the air that comes off the Mississippi. It gets in a Memphian's soul. Your mother was Memphis born and bred. She had trouble adjusting to life in Princeton, and your father was a stubborn, unbending man. I think he feared the pull of this city on your mother . . . jealousy, in a way, but not because of those foolish, unfounded Elvis rumors . . . and so he became dogmatic, unwilling to be flexible."

"She left my father," Clay gritted out.

Marion shook her head vigorously from side to side. "Clare wasn't giving up on your father. She had every intention of returning home. If it hadn't been for the fire . . . " Her eyes filled with tears as she spoke. She swiped at them with a tissue and pointed to an envelope in the box of miscellany.

Clay picked it up and immediately noticed the airline logo on the outside of the envelope. Inside was a thirty-two-year-old, one-way ticket, Memphis to Newark. It was too much to digest at once. Clay stood abruptly and headed for the door.

"Mr. Jessup, where are you going? We have a meeting soon."

He waved a hand dismissively. "I'm going for a walk. I need to think."

"But what should I tell the lawyers?"

"Tell them . . . tell them . . . the deal is off . . . for now."

Like minds and all that...

It was Christmas Eve and Clay was driving a bright red Jeep Cherokee up the lane to Sweet Hollow Farm, more hopeful and frightened than he'd ever been in all his life.

Would he and Annie be able to work things out?

Would her brothers come out with shotguns in hand?

Would he fight to the death for her . . . a virtual knight in shining Jeep?

Would Annie still love him in the end?

There was a full moon out tonight, but Clay didn't need it, or the Jeep's headlights, to see. The entire barn and farmhouse were outlined with Christmas tree lights. In the front yard was a plywood Santa and reindeer display, highlighted by floodlights. The whole scene resembled a farm version of Chevy Chase's movie "National Lampoon's Christmas Vacation." He wondered idly who had climbed up on the roofs of the house and barn to put up all those blasted lights. Probably Annie. Or Aunt Liza. Damn!

Clay was so nervous he could barely think straight, especially when he saw the front door open, even before he emerged from the vehicle.

It was Annie.

Please, God, he prayed, *no big toes this time.*

"Clay?" Annie said, coming down the steps and walking woodenly toward him. She looked as if she'd been crying.

Who made her cry? I'll kill the person who made her cry?

Oh! It was probably me.

"Where did you get the Jeep?" she asked nervously, as if that irrelevant detail was the most important thing on her mind.

"I . . . uh . . . kind of . . . uh . . . rented it." Clay's brain was stuck in first gear.

"You came back," she said then, surrendering to a sob. "I called the hotel all night and Marion said you were gone, and I thought . . . I thought you went home."

"I am home, sweetheart." Clay opened his arms to her and gathered her close. "I've done a lot of walking, and thinking, since you left me."

"I've been so miserable," she blubbered against his neck.

"Me, too, sweetheart. Me, too." He was running his hands over her back, her arms, her hair, her back again. He kissed the top of her head, her wet cheeks, her lips. He tried to show her with soul-deep kisses how much he'd missed her, and how important she was to him. He couldn't get enough of her. He was afraid to let go for fear this was all a dream.

Annie leaned back to get a better look at him. Cupping his face in her hands, she gazed at him, tears streaming down her cheeks, with such open love that Clay felt blessed.

"Annie-love, we're going to work this out. I've talked with my legal department in New York, and they see no problem with my setting up a satellite office in Memphis. Could you live with me in New Jersey part of the time, if I'm willing to live here?"

Her mouth had dropped open with surprise. "You would do that for me?"

"In a heartbeat." *It was either that, or suffer a heartbreak. Easy choice!*

"How about the hotel?"

"Well, I'm not sure. I called a Memphis entrepreneur this morning. This guy has the capital to finance a purchase of the hotel property, and he has the Memphis ties that would make such a landmark attractive to him. But I don't know if I'm ready to give up the hotel yet. Oh, Annie, I've learned some things this week about my mother and father that are going to take me a long time to accept."

She pressed a light kiss to his lips in understanding. "We don't have to decide all this right now."

"*We?*" he asked hopefully.

"*We,*" she repeated.

"Will you marry me, Annie-love?"

"In a heartbeat," she said, echoing Clay's phrase.

A short time later, they were heading toward the front steps, arms wrapped around each other's waists, their progress hampered by his limp and their constant stopping to kiss and murmur soft words of love.

Clay couldn't stop grinning.

"You're looking awfully self-satisfied, Mr. Jessup."

Sandra Hill

"Well, I'm a negotiator, Annie. It's part of my business as a venture capitalist. I figure I just pulled off the deal of the century. I got you, didn't I, babe?"

She laughed. "You had me anyhow, *babe*. I already talked to my brothers about taking over the farm so I could move to New Jersey. Why do you think I was calling you all night?" She tapped him playfully on the chin in one-upmanship.

"Well, you little witch, you," Clay said. But what he thought was, *Wait till you see what I bought at the mall. You haven't had the last word yet.*

He never knew there could be such joy in giving...

Elvis was singing "Blue Christmas" on the stereo, a fire was roaring in the fireplace, the tree lights were flickering, and Clay was enjoying his first ever family Christmas Eve celebration. If his heart expanded with any more joy, it just might explode.

It was almost midnight, but still the family members were opening their Christmas gifts. Clay sat on the sofa with Annie on his one side, holding his hand. Aunt Liza was on the other side, keeping an eagle eye on his hands, lest they stray.

The gifts they gave to each other were simple items, some homemade, some silly, many downright practical. Who knew that people got socks and underwear for Christmas gifts! Johnny raved over his new athletic shoes . . . the spiffiest in the store, according to Annie. Everyone received new shirts and jeans. The pearl stud earrings that Johnny bought for Annie, probably from Walmart, might have come from Cartier's, for all her oohing and aahing. And the boys exhibited just as much appreciation over cheap card games or music cassettes.

There were even gifts for Clay from the family, to his surprise and slight embarrassment. When Aunt Liza handed him a small box, wrapped with Santa Claus paper, he almost choked. *She wouldn't!*

Aunt Liza tsked at him till he unwrapped it to find a CD of "Elvis's Greatest Hits."

"Whadja think I bought, you fool?" she said with a chuckle.

Chet, Roy and Hank pooled their money to get him a pair of low-heeled cowboy boots. Jerry Lee gave him a Wall Street joke book, and Johnny presented him with a tie imprinted with dozens of Holstein cows.

When it was Annie's turn, she made much ado over the homemade tree ornament with his name and date stenciled on the back, thus

74

symbolizing his formal acceptance into her family. Finally, with much nervousness, she handed him what he sensed must be a special gift.

Tears filled his eyes, and he couldn't speak at first. Inside was a leather album. The words on front, embossed with gold letters, said, "The Works of Clare Gannett." Annie had somehow managed to gather together dozens of photographs made by his mother. On the last page was a copy of an obituary from a Memphis newspaper, detailing her artistic talent and what she had contributed to Memphis and music history in her short life.

"Where did you get these?" he asked when his emotions were finally under control.

"I badgered the museum curator yesterday. When he heard your story, he helped me pull those photos made by your mother and duplicated them at a one-hour photo studio down the street."

"Thank you, love," he whispered against her hair. Then, he decided it was time to reciprocate. "Can you guys help me get some gifts from the Jeep?"

Annie's brothers gasped out a single-word curse when they saw how the back of the Jeep overflowed with gaily wrapped packages, some them in huge boxes.

Aunt Liza could be heard rapping on the kitchen window at that crude expletive. "I heard that, boys. You're not too old for soap, you know. That goes for you, too, Mr. Jessup."

After three trips, the living room was filled with his purchases. Hank closed the door with a shiver—it was turning cold outside and snowflakes had just begun to flutter down in wonderful Christmas fashion—and he asked Clay, "Where'd you buy that spiffy red Jeep?"

"Oh, he didn't buy it," Annie explained. "It's a rental."

"That sure looked like a new car plate to me," Hank commented as he hung his coat on an old-fashioned coat rack.

"Clay?" Annie tilted her head in question to him. "Did you buy yourself a Jeep?"

"Well, no, I didn't buy a Jeep for *myself*."

Everyone turned to stare at him then. Clay shifted uneasily, and his eyes wandered over to Hank.

There was a long telling silence. Then Hank whooped, "Me? *Me?* You bought a car for me?"

"Clay Jessup! You can't go out and buy a car for someone you barely know for a Christmas present."

"I can't?" he asked, honestly perplexed. "Well, hell . . . I mean, heck, Annie, Hank distinctly said that first night I was here for dinner that if he had as much money as me, he would buy a fancy new vehicle and be the biggest chick magnet in the United States. I knew you'd be upset if I bought him a Jaguar."

"Holy Cow! I wonder what I get if Hank gets a new Jeep," Johnny commented in an awestruck voice.

Annie made a low gurgling sound, which he figured was his cue to move on to the other gifts.

Chet's Adam's apple moved awkwardly as he studied Clay's gift . . . airline tickets for Chet Fallon and son, Jason, for London, dated December 26.

"At least you show *some* good sense," Aunt Liza observed. "It's about time someone pushed Chet in the right direction."

For the entire family, Clay bought a high-tech computer system that would allow them to program in all the statistics on their milk production. Aunt Liza got a microwave which she pooh-poohed at first, stating "What would I do with one of those fancy contraptions?" But she was soon reading the manual exclaiming, "Didja know you can do preserves in a microwave?" By the time Jerry Lee went ballistic over his laptop, Roy had gone speechless over the bank envelope showing a trust fund passbook covering his entire vet school tuition, and Johnny was in tears over a new entertainment system for his bedroom, complete with portable TV, CD player and game system . . . well, by then Annie had given up on her protests.

"It's too much, Clay," she said on a sigh of frustration.

"No, it's not, Annie. Generosity is giving till it hurts . . . like you and your family do every Christmas. This is just money I spent here . . . money whose loss I won't even miss."

"But I still think you should take back—"

"Annie," Aunt Liza cautioned in a stern voice, "shut up."

They all laughed at that.

"So what did you get for Annie?" Hank wanted to know.

She gazed at the ring on her finger. "I have my gift."

But Hank ignored her. "With all the great gifts he gave us, he must have bought you at least . . . a new barn. Ha, ha, ha!"

Annie folded her arms indignantly over her chest at the teasing, and Clay's face heated up in a too-telling fashion.

"Well, actually . . . ," he admitted, handing her a gift certificate from a local contracting firm.

"You didn't!" Annie scolded.

He did. It was a purchase order for a new barn roof.

She punched him in the stomach, but he didn't care. He could see the love in her eyes.

There are benefits to being down on the farm...

A hour later, everyone had gone to bed, except him and Annie.

"I love you, Annie," he said for what must be the hundredth time that evening.

"I love you, too, Clay . . . so much that my heart feels as if it's overflowing."

"It's hard to believe that so much has happened to us in the short time since we first met."

"Maybe you were destined to come to Tennessee . . . for us to meet. Maybe there *is* an Elvis spirit looking over Memphis."

Clay wanted to balk at the idea, but the words wouldn't come out. "Maybe you're right. Perhaps Elvis really does live," he finally conceded. "Oh, I forgot. There's one more gift I bought for you." He reached behind the sofa and handed her the package.

"Clay, this is too much. You've already given me too much."

"Well, actually, this gift is for me." He waggled his eyebrows at her.

Hesitantly, Annie unwrapped the package that came from a costume shop in the mall. Annie laughed when she lifted the lid. It was a Daisy Mae outfit—white, off-the-shoulder blouse, and cut-off jeans that were cut off *real* high on the buttock. "You devil, you."

"So, are you going to try it on for me tonight?"

"Here?"

"Hell, no. In the hayloft."

Carrying on tradition...

There is an old legend that says on Christmas Eve on a farm, the animals talk.

One thing is certain. On this Christmas Eve, on Sweet Valley Farm, the animals in the barn, under the hayloft, had a lot to talk about.

Author's Note

If you believe the spirit of Elvis is still "alive," you're not alone.

It's been more than thirty years since "The King" died, but almost six hundred Elvis fan clubs still flourish around the world. No one disputes the fact that Elvis had a profound impact on the music industry, but his magic lives on not only in his own songs, but those of the many musicians influenced by his talent.

So, if you are one of those people who can't help singing along when an Elvis tune comes on the radio . . . or if a smile breaks out when you hear "Blue Suede Shoes" . . . or if you believe some people "live on" after death, then you're not alone.

One thing is for sure, the legend does go on.

Jinx Christmas

Chapter One

It's amazing what you can find in a supermarket today . . .

Brenda Caslow was standing in the personal products aisle of the A & P when she heard the first scream.

It was immediately followed by another scream, then shouts of:

"It's him! Omigod, It's him!"

"Hurry, Ralph, buy a camera."

"Whoa! He is hot."

"Maybe he'll sign my t-shirt."

"Maybe he'll sign my bra."

That's all Brenda needed to hear. She knew what it was . . . rather, who it was. The louse must have tracked her to the grocery store. Lance Caslow, her ex-husband.

He sauntered up to her and smiled. Probably figured one smile and she'd be melting at his feet, right here under the suppositories and . . . oh, no! . . . condoms.

Actually, his smile did make her melt. Always had. Ever since they were kids, riding their tricycles down the neighborhood sidewalk. Lance had shown his competitive spirit even then; he'd always insisted she had to race him, and he always won. She'd had to give up her stash of Tootsie Roll Pops then as a prize. Later, she gave up lots more.

They got married right out of high school, had been together for nine years before she got pregnant, and were divorced three years later. A lot of history there.

And, hot damn, giving him a quick head-to-toe survey, she could see why women flocked all over him, and not just because he was a NASCAR superhero. He was tall . . . well, six foot to her five-six. He had dark blond hair, spritzed up right now into one of those silly styles that looked as if it had been combed with a mixer, classic facial features, a golden tan, and a body to die for with not an ounce of fat. She should be so lucky. On a perpetual diet, Brenda had more curves than a Slinky. In fact, she'd been about to buy some diet pills. Not that they ever worked.

"Hey, babe," he said casually, as if he showed up in the A & P on a regular basis. More like, never. He leaned forward to give her a kiss.

She turned her head, and his lips met her cheek. Even that caused little ripples of pleasure to ricochet through her body in anticipation of more. *Not gonna happen.*

"Are you stalking me?"

"Me?" He slapped a hand over his heart in mock affront.

Then he grew more serious. "It's the only way I can get you to talk to me."

"We have nothing to say."

"Yeah, we do." He tugged at one of the blonde curls framing her face, the bane of her life. "Your hair looks different. Nice."

"Highlights."

"I like it. Oh, no!" He took the box that she still clutched in her hand. "Diet pills! You aren't still obsessing over your weight, are you? Believe me, you look great just the way you are."

"Hah! I'm always going to be a size ten, when the ideal is a size six. I'm always going to have curves, when slim is in. I'm getting older, and your girlfriends are getting younger."

"I'm the same age you are, and thirty-five isn't old. As for your curves, I love each and every one of them."

And he did. Brenda knew that. He had adored her body, with all its imperfections. "Listen, I don't have time for this."

"You still working for that treasure hunting company? Jinxed?" He was stalling for time.

"Not Jinxed. Jinx, as in Jinx, Inc. And the answer is yes."

"You ever gonna come back to NASCAR to work in the pits?"

Brenda was a top notch mechanic. When Lance had first gone to Indiana to start racing, she'd gone along as a mechanic. Women had been dogging him then, too, but she'd been there to put the kibosh on any hanky panky.

"How did you find me?"

"Uh . . . "

"You rat. You've been pumping Patti again, haven't you?" Patti was their seven-year-old daughter.

"It didn't take much pumping." The little rascal, like many other casualties of divorce, adored her father and wanted them to get back together again.

Just then, they noticed the crowd that had gathered at both ends of the aisle, craning their necks to see them, creeping closer and closer as newcomers pushed from the back. They were mostly quiet, watching. Some were flashing disposable cameras.

Damn! I'll probably see us on the cover of The Star next week.

"Hey, folks, great to see ya." It was amazing to watch Lance morph into his celebrity persona. "I'll sign some autographs if you move yourselves out to the parking lot, in an orderly fashion. I've gotta talk to my wife here."

Where did he learn to handle a crowd like that? Certainly not growing up in Perth Amboy. He gained polish over the years. I gained weight.

He put an arm around her shoulders, and squeezed.

She squirmed out of his embrace. Being that close to Lance was dangerous. "I'm not his wife," she yelled out, but no one was listening. The herd was rushing to the parking lot to get the best positions. "Anymore," she added more weekly.

"Semantics," he commented.

She and Lance had divorced five years ago. It had not been pretty. Lance had to be dragged kicking and screaming into court. Even then, he'd told the judge he didn't want a divorce. Unfortunately, actions spoke louder than words.

"I still feel like your husband. I still wear my wedding band. C'mon, Brendie, let's go somewhere and talk. I can't be charming in the middle of fifty types of sanitary napkins."

She hated that he called her Brendie, mainly because she used to love the way he called her Brendie. He would whisper that name when he . . . *I am not going there. No way!* "You could be charming in the middle of a pig sty, covered with hog doo-doo, and you know it."

He shrugged. "Have dinner with me. Or a drink. Yeah, drinks would be good."

She had to smile. "So you can get me drunk and have your way with me?"

"God, yes!"

"Lance," she said with a whooshy exhale, "how many women have you made love to?"

"Ever?" He was clearly shocked to be put on such a wide spot.

"Ever?"

"None."

"Puh-leeze!"

"You said making love. I've had sex with lots of women, but I only ever made love with one. You."

"Semantics," she repeated his own word back at him. "You and Bill Clinton oughta form a club."

"You believed everything you read in those tabloids, honey, and they just weren't true."

"I know that, but pictures don't lie. And that blonde bimbo was sitting on your lap with her hand on your butt right smack dab on the front page of the *National Enquirer.*"

"Pictures lie, too."

"You're giving me a headache. We have been over this so many times."

"I never, ever, cheated on you while we were together."

"Obviously, you and I have different definitions of cheating. And, by the way, I notice your careful choice of words. 'While we were together.' How about while we were married but separated?"

His face flushed. "I was angry."

"I was angry, too."

"Okay, I was stupid."

"That was never in doubt."

"Give me another chance, baby."

"No." She saw the grief on his face, this man that she knew so well. But he had hurt her so badly. Over and over. His celebrity had become more important than her. And the groupies . . . there were all those beautiful women just waiting to jump in bed with the winner of the next Brickhouse, or Daytona, or race du jour.

"I love you."

Oh, that was a low blow, especially when he said it with tears welling in his eyes.

"I don't love you anymore," she lied. "I don't even like you."

"Yeah, you do. Give me fifteen minutes in a private room, and I'll prove it to you."

"You are such a . . . a toad."

"Yeah, well, you must have a taste for pond scum because there was a time when you enjoyed licking me all over. It's a wonder you don't have warts on your tongue."

She knew he spoke from pride and disappointment. That didn't excuse his crudity. "You jerk!"

"I love you, too, baby."

She grabbed hold of her own short curls and tugged with frustration. "Aaarrgh! You're driving me crazy."

"I take that as a good sign."

"You're delusional."

"I'm not giving up, Brendie. And you know why?"

She was probably going to regret this, but she asked, "Why?"

"Because of this." He pulled her into his arms and wouldn't let go, even when she smacked him on his shoulders and the side of his head. Then he lowered his mouth to hers, open-mouthed and hungry. He devoured her with his never-ending kiss till she softened with a moan of surrender and opened her mouth to his, kissing him back with a traitorous fervor. When he finally released her, she had to hold onto the grocery cart or risk melting to the floor in an erotic puddle.

To give him credit, he didn't smirk or make a gloating remark. Instead, he used his thumb to caress her bottom lip and said in a raw voice, "That's why I'm not giving up, babe."

With those words, he walked off.

And she wondered how she was going to withstand his next assault, never doubting he would try again. And again. And again.

Me and WHO? . . .

Lance was walking away from Brenda with a mixture of elation and bone-deep disappointment.

Elation because she still loved him. He knew she did.

And disappointment because she was grinding him down with all the rejections. Nothing he did seemed to work. Nothing. Five years of cajoling, apologizing, teasing, and begging. What did he get for his efforts? Nada.

He was passing by the checkout lines, heading toward the crowd outside when he stopped and did a double take. Holy shit! He saw himself staring out from one of the tabloids . . . with a freakin' half-dressed starlet with enormous breasts. It looked as if she had her hand on his crotch.

He had no idea if he'd been at the same party that the starlet had—you'd think he would remember that—or if some enterprising editor had done a cut and paste job. All he knew was that he'd never been with that particular goddess of silicone, in any way. But if Brenda saw this picture, it would be five years ago, all over again.

So, he did what any half-brained guy would do. He bought every issue of the tabloid before he left the store.

Desperate men do desperate things . . .

"I'm desperate," Lance Caslow said later that night, and almost fell off his chair at the Loosey Goosey Bar, somewhere in California . . . he wasn't exactly sure where.

"Nah. Yer jist drunk, thass what you are," his best friend and fellow NASCAR driver Easy Eddie Morgan slurred out, even as he tried to wink, but just grimaced at a buxom blonde waitress who should own stock in a push-up bra company.

"We're both drunk," Lance concluded. "Knee-walking, shit-faced, we-oughta-go-home blitzed. Can you remember why?"

"I think we mighta won the Brickhouse, or placed, or somethin'. No, no, no. That was last summer. We were doin' a commercial. In L.A."

"Oh, that's right."

"So, why are ya desperate, good buddy?"

"I'm so in love with my ex-wife it hurts, right here." He pressed a forefinger to his abdomen, though he'd been aiming at his heart. "But she won't take me back."

Easy shrugged. "Ex-wives are a dime a dozen. Find another one." Easy should know, he had three of them and was paying alimony out the wazoo.

Lance shook his head. "I don't want anyone else and haven't for a long, long time. Brenda and I go way back, to elementary school. I thought we would be together forever." He didn't even care how corny that sounded.

"And?"

He sighed. "I screwed up. Bigtime."

"Didja say yer sorry?"

He nodded.

"Didja buy her jewelry to make up fer it?"

"Yes. She threw the damn necklace in my face."

"Flowers?"

"A pigload. She gave them to the old folks' home."

"Well, that leaves only one thing. Beg."

"I tried that, too."

Easy looped an arm over his shoulder. "I hate ta break it to ya but she might not love ya anymore."

Lance shook his head slowly, and then he shook it harder from side to side till a headache began to jackhammer right behind his eyes. "She loves me, all right. She just doesn't trust me any farther than she can throw me."

"Ya need a plan. Ya need outside help."

"Where's a matchmaker when you need one? Ha, ha, ha!"

"Yeah, hire yerself a yenta. Ha, ha, ha!" Easy sometimes lapsed into his Jewish heritage; so, he knew words like that.

A tiny little idea burrowed into his pathetic brain. A matchmaker? "Hmmmm."

"What?"

"Remember that wedding I went to?"

"The one with the ex-Amish Navy SEAL?"

"That would be the one. Anyhow, there was this crazy old Cajun lady there. She was spoutin' stuff 'bout St. Jude and hope chests and thunderbolts of love."

"Man, yer really drunk," Easy slurred out.

"I'm goin' to Loo-zee-anna," he announced. "Southern Loo-zee-anna. Bayou Black, to be precise."

"Yer big plan is to get a matchmaker?"

"Yep! Her name is Tante Lulu."

Shopping . . . the cure for every girl's woes . . .

"Are you sure you don't want to sit on Santa's lap?"

"Mom!" Brenda's daughter Patti said, gazing at her with horror. Patti—seven, going on seventeen—quickly glanced around her at the mall to see if anyone had heard her mother's embarrassing remark. "That is so uncool!"

"Well, excuse me, for not being cool." Brenda squeezed her daughter's thin shoulders to show she wasn't offended. "In the past . . . last year, for heaven's sake . . . you gave Santa your Christmas wish list."

"I was a child then," Patti said. "Besides, *Santa* already knows what I want for Christmas." She gave Brenda a pointed look to let her know who the Santa in question was.

Brenda wasn't even going to react to that wish remark and spoil their post-Thanksgiving trip to the massive Woodbridge Mall, a virtual city of stores, restaurants, and entertainment. Patti's wish was the same every year anyhow. "Dear Santa: Please let Mommy and Daddy make up so we can be a family again."

Brenda hated it, that Patti no longer believed in Santa Claus, that she was growing up so fast, and that she still hoped for a reconciliation between her and Lance. With each year, Patti looked more like her

Daddy. Dark blonde hair, perfect features, a beauty in the making. She shared Lance's sense of style, too. The outfit she'd chosen for the day: a twirly red and green plaid skirt, a red turtle neck, a short pink fake fur jacket, white knee-highs, black patent leather shoes and a sparkly hair clip. She'd inherited her father's gift of charm, as well, as indicated by her next observation.

"You know, Mom, you are so beautiful. It's no wonder Daddy loves you so much."

"Give me a break!"

"Really, he does love you. He tells everyone."

"Oh, yeah?"

"Yep, he told me again before he went . . . uh, I mean . . . uh, before he went on his trip."

Brenda recognized a slip of the tongue when she heard it, especially from her too-transparent daughter. "What trip?"

"I don't know." Patti's cute little pixie face bloomed pink.

"Patti?"

"It's a secret trip, and that's all I can say. Okay?"

"A secret trip? He better not be buying you another outrageously expensive Christmas gift." Last year he'd given her an electric mini-sports car that exactly matched the vehicle he'd used when he won the Daytona the year before. It probably cost ten thousand dollars.

"The trip has nothing to do with me. And that's all I'm gonna say. You wanna get a soft pretzel and a drink, or . . . ?" Patti's eyes twinkled with mischief.

"Or what?"

"Or we could go into Victoria's Secret and buy you one of those see-through nighties. Betcha Dad would like that."

Yep, her daughter was growing up way too fast.

Chapter Two

Even desperate men draw the line at . . .

Lance was cruising along U.S. 90 out of Houma, Louisiana. He passed a few sugar plantations on the way, some decrepit shacks and houseboats, and modest bayou-side homes. Some of them still showed damage from Hurricane Katrina, even after all these years.

He was heading for a cottage on Bayou Black that he had pinpointed on his GPS system. It was the home of Louise Rivard, better known as Tante Lulu, matchmaker extraordinaire.

This is the dumbest thing I've ever done, and I've done some really dumb things.

Like losing Brenda? a voice in his head said.

Yep, the dumbest.

The weather was a balmy seventy degrees . . . balmy, considering that this was December. But then, this was the Southland. Despite the weather, he wasn't about to put the top down on his Lexus convertible, the least flashy of his fifteen automobiles. Even wearing sunglasses and a baseball cap, he'd been recognized occasionally when he stopped for gas on the three hundred mile trip from his home in Texas. Publicity was the last thing he needed on this desperate mission.

"This must be it," he murmured, pulling into the driveway of a small cottage covered with logs accented by white-washed chinking. A wide porch, with several wooden rockers, faced a stretch of stream . . . well, a bayou, actually. That's what they called alligator-infested creeks here in Louisiana.

"Son of a bitch!" he said aloud. There *was* a real live gator sunning itself right in the old lady's yard.

Swamps and thick jungle-like vegetation ruled in this region, but the cottage had neatly trimmed grass and colorful flowerbeds in cleared areas on all four sides. He smiled when he recognized the plastic and plaster statues placed in various spots among the flowers. St. Jude. Tante Lulu's favorite saint, he recalled. In fact, last time he'd seen her at Caleb Peachy's wedding in Central Pennsylvania a few months back, she'd shoved a miniature statue into his hand and told him, "It's fer hopeless cases . . . like yours."

He gave the gator another wary look and shivered with distaste. Lance had a pistol under his front seat that he kept for security reasons. *Should I shoot the bugger? Nah! I'll just run like hell if the beast comes after me.*

No sooner did he step out of his car . . . carefully, with an eye on the walking pocketbook . . . than Tante Lulu stepped out onto her porch. "Welcome, *cher*, welcome! Come make yerself at home, you. I gots gumbo on the simmer and a strong cup of Cajun coffee hot enough ta burn yer tongue."

"Uh . . . what about that alligator over there." At the moment said gator was ambling towards them.

"Oh, thass jist Useless."

"He might be useless, but he has sharp teeth."

"Useless is his name, honey. He usta be Remy's pet gator, but then Remy moved off his houseboat and Useless moved down the bayou to live by me. He likes ta eat cheese doodles. Ya gots any cheese doodles in yer car?"

"No, I'm fresh out of cheese doodles." *An alligator named Useless who eats snack food. Okay.*

"Remy usta give him moon pies, but he'd get on such a sugar high, he even scared the other gators. And he was gettin' fat. So, we changed ta cheese doodles."

This is real interesting, but . . .

"This is real interestin', Lance, but we gots work ta do. Reach down here, boy, and gimme some sugar."

Lance was six foot tall. Tante Lulu was about five foot zero. Bending was in fact a necessity. When he did lean down, and she gave him a warm hug, followed by a kiss on both cheeks, he felt an odd sort of warmth rush through him. He suddenly knew he'd done the right thing coming to the old lady for help.

"Did you feel that?" he asked.

"Feel what, honey?"

"That shot of . . . I don't know . . . electricity, heat, something?"

She patted him on the hand. "Thass jist St. Jude workin' through me. And doan be givin' me that disbelievin' look. Ya want help, ya gotta believe."

They entered the cottage, whose low ceiling barely missed hitting the top of Lance's head. The living room was cozy, with a Christmas tree sitting in one corner with its lights blinking, fake holly draped over a fireplace mantle, kitchy Santa's and elves, mixed in with St. Jude statues, on every table surface, and Christmas music coming out of an old fashioned console type record player ... Cajun Christmas music, a mixture of French and English. The walls were adorned with a couple dozen framed photographs. Her nephews, he supposed ... Luc, Remy, René and Tee-John, her niece Charmaine, and their various spouses and children. There were lots of them. He'd met most of them at Caleb's wedding; Caleb was a member of the Jinx treasure hunting team, along with Brenda.

"Come, you, sit yer purty self down," she said, leading him into her kitchen, which was a step back in time ... to the 1940s, he would guess. Enamel table, metal chairs with red Naugahyde cushioned seats, a wide porcelain sink under a window with red and white checkered curtains. Dried spices hung from the ceiling, giving the room a wonderful aroma, accented by the delicious odors coming from a pot cooking on the stove. It was a pleasant room. Martha Stewart, despite her high tech kitchens, would love this place.

The kitchen, in fact the whole house, held ambiance. Lance laughed to himself, that he would even know such a word. Hell, it's what his decorator had said when designing his home in Houston, and it was cold as steel compared to this. Brenda would love this.

That thought brought him to the point of this visit. But before he could speak, Tante Lulu placed a bowl of gumbo, several slices of warm bread and butter, and a mug of coffee in front of him, with the words, "*Bon appetit!*" Then said, out of the blue, "Do you know Richard Simmons?"

"Ummm, this is good," he said, taking his first bite of the thick, Cajun, stew-like dish. "Do you mean Richard Simmons, the exercise nut?"

Tante Lulu inhaled sharply and slapped him on the shoulder with a dish towel. "Shame on you. Richard ain't a nut. He's a hunk. If I was younger, I'd go after him, guaranteed."

"Okaaaay." *Someone's nuts around here, but I don't know if it's me, Richard Simmons, or this Cajun fruitcake here.* But he was raised to be polite. "You're not that old."

Tante Lulu laughed. "Sweetie, I'm so old I coulda been a waitress at the Last Supper. Not that I don't still have some snap in my garters."

No way was he going to step in that minefield. "This is really good." He hadn't realized he was so hungry and didn't even protest when Tante Lulu refilled his bowl without asking.

"You sure are good lookin', boy. Purtier than a speckled pup. Betcha the wimmen chase ya lak crazy. Betcha think yer hotter 'n a pig's butt in a pepper patch."

"I *do not* think I'm hotter than . . . what you said."

"Well, dontcha be havin' a hissy fit. There ain't that many men as hot as Richard."

"Richard Petty?"

"No, aintcha been listenin'? Richard Simmons. Mebbe ya know someone who knows him and ya kin invite Richard to the Lance Caslow and the Cajun Bad Boys show?"

Lance sputtered into his coffee. "Huh?"

She narrowed her eyes at him. "I'm a *traiteur* . . . a healer . . . but that doan mean I have special afro-diss-aks in my pocket. Ya weren't thinkin' I had a magic bullet here for ya, were ya? Iffen thass the case, ya might as well skedaddle on home. Even juju tea takes a while ta work."

"They make tea from Jujyfruits candy?"

"Boy, yer thicker 'n a bayou stump. But dontcha be worryin' none. We's fixin' ta get yer wife back fer ya, lickedy split. Brenda won't even know the thunderbolt hit her."

"Whoa, whoa, whoa! Let's backtrack about a NASCAR mile here, sweetheart."

"Oooh, thass a good touch, that sweetheart thang. Betcha the wimmen swoon over that."

Yeah, but not Brenda. "What show?"

"I already tol' ya. The Cajun Bad Boys."

"I'm not Cajun."

She waved a hand dismissively. "We'll make ya an honorary Cajun."

"We *who*?"

Within seconds, he found out *who* as Tante Lulu's four nephews, and the niece Charmaine, showed up in ten and fifteen minute intervals.

"Hey, Lance." It was John LeDeux greeting him as he strolled in carrying a mondo size bag of cheese doodles, the size you buy in surplus warehouses. John, better known as Tee-John to his family, had been a member of the Jinx treasure hunting crew but was now a cop in Fontaine, Louisiana. "Guess my aunt roped you in, too." He grinned as if Lance was the sucker of the month, which he probably was.

"Didja bring Lance's hope chest?"

"Oh, yeah!" He pointed to a pine box out on the porch.

"A . . . a hope chest? For me?"

"*Oui.* I gives 'em ta all the men before I fixes up their love life. Ya want the 'L & B' embroidery on the pillow cases ta be in green or blue?"

"Wait till you see the pot holders she made you out of NASCAR flags," John told him, not even trying to suppress a chuckle. "And the bride quilt with checkered flags alternating with hearts. And a monogrammed toilet paper holder. And the St. Jude flag to put on your race car."

Now that last he wouldn't mind. A racer needed all the help he could get.

"Doan pay no nevermind ta Tee-John. He'll be gettin' his hope chest sometime soon."

"No, no, no!" John was turning a lovely shade of gray that gave Lance immense pleasure.

"How's the police work going?" he asked.

John shrugged. "Beats pickin' cotton, or . . . " He cast his aunt a mischievous grin, " . . . or strippin'."

The old lady smacked her nephew, whom she clearly adored, on his arm. "Doan mind Tee-John," she told Lance. "This one, bless his heart, thinks the sun comes up ta hear him crow."

"Doesn't it?" the young man asked with mock innocence.

The niece Charmaine came next, carrying outdoor Christmas decorations that they were all apparently going to help the old lady put up. Charmaine looked like a Christmas ornament herself, with huge teased black hair, earrings that dangled a bunch of colored bells, red spandex pants, white high heeled cowboy boots, a green silk, long-sleeved t-shirt with the words "Don't Tangle With me", and in smaller print "Charmaine's Beauty Spa." She was what his friend Easy would call a Hootchie Mama and mean it as a compliment. His daughter Patti, a real girly girl, would love Charmaine.

Luc and Remy LeDeux came next, also carting Christmas decorations and a bushel of okra. What anyone would do with a bushel of okra, he had no idea. Luc was the oldest of the LeDeux brothers, a lawyer. Remy, badly scarred in Desert Storm, was a pilot.

After they shook hands with him and asked a few questions about his latest race—people in the South loved NASCAR—they all sat down at the table. Tante Lulu placed mugs of coffee in front of all of them, along with a platter of fresh-baked beignets, a Louisiana delicacy.

Lance was feeling a mite embarrassed . . . okay, a lot embarrassed. When he'd called Tante Lulu to ask for her help, he didn't know she would be calling in the troops to share his secret shame. Lance Caslow, celebrity playboy, couldn't get his wife back on his own.

"Tell us what the problem is, Lance, and we'll see what we can do to help," Charmaine advised. "And don't be blushin'. We've all been in the same boat."

I doubt that. Taking a deep breath, he began. "I have loved Brenda forever. We grew up together. We married right after high school. We have a little girl together. I thought we would be together always."

"I hear a great big but in there," Remy said.

"I screwed up."

Charmaine and Tante Lulu both glowered at him.

"I didn't cheat on her," he protested.

The two women arched their eyebrows.

"I didn't cheat on her while we were together."

The men laughed.

"Listen, my friend, I'm a lawyer," Luc said, "but you don't need to be a lawyer to know that terminology doesn't give you the wiggle room you think it does."

"Yeah, I know. That's what Brenda said. I'm about ready to give up. This is my last shot. Really, it feels hopeless."

"What a load of hooey!" Tante Lulu said. "But ya came ta the right place fer hopeless cases." She squeezed his shoulder and passed him another beignet. "When didja first start havin' troubles and when did ya get a divorce?" Tante Lulu wanted to know.

"There was trouble almost from the get-go . . . or once I started winning some races. The groupies, the parties, the drinking. But as long as Brenda was with me, we were okay. She was a NASCAR mechanic for my team. But then we had Patti . . . our little girl is seven now . . . and Brenda couldn't go on the road as much. I guess I let all the attention go to my head. I didn't actually do anything, but—"

"Sonny, let's get one thing straight. A man, he can be slicker 'n deer guts on a doorknob, but excuses doan make the gumbo boil. Cheatin' is cheatin', whether it be lookin', or kissin', or rentin' a room at the Hidey Hole Hotel. As Doctor Phil would say, ya gotta own the problem."

Lance's jaw dropped at Tante Lulu's little sermon. The rest of them just grinned, probably having heard that sermon a few dozen times.

"I admit, I made mistakes. Big mistakes. Number one, I let myself be photographed with hot women in compromising positions. Number two, I didn't go home immediately and beg Brenda to forgive me. Instead, I said she was overly jealous. Number three, when we were separated, I got drunk and had a one-night stand with a groupie who sold the story to the National Enquirer. Number four, I let my pride rule way too long. Now Brenda won't even talk to me."

"Tsk, tsk, tsk!" Tante Lulu said.

"Here I thought you were gonna say that yer problem was yer needle dick," John teased.

"Tee-John LeDeux! You got a mouth like a Bourbon Street pimp. I kin still whomp yer fanny," Tante Lulu scolded. "And it ain't polite to make fun of a man's doo-doo."

John just winked at his aunt.

"That's okay. Brenda told that needle dick story about my . . . uh, doo-doo . . . for a long time, to get back at me," Lance explained.

"Did it work?" Remy asked.

"Hell, yes. Try explaining to people that you don't have a needle dick without dropping your drawers."

"Men and the size of their you-know-whats!" Charmaine said to Tante Lulu. "If they'd stop worrying about size and stop thinking with their zippers, women would be all over them like white gravy on a warm biscuit."

"The big question is: does Brenda still love you?" The old lady might act a bit ditzy, but she knew how to get at the heart of things.

"Yes," he said without hesitation. "She just doesn't like me very much."

Two hours later—hope chest stowed in his back seat, St. Jude statue in his pocket, and a Tupperware container of gumbo in the trunk—Lance left, shaking his head with dismay. He'd just agreed to the most outlandish plan to get Brenda back.

The NASCAR Bad Boy had officially become a Cajun Bad Boy.

And then he threw out the hook . . .

Brenda studied the card that had come in the mail today, addressed to Brenda and Patti Caslow. It was a formal invitation on heavy cream parchment with a holly border.

You are cordially invited to
A CAJUN CHRISTMAS DINNER REVUE
at
The Southern Louisiana Civic Center
honoring
NASCAR DRIVER LANCE CASLOW
Entertainment by The Cajun Bad Boys
Proceeds to benefit Our Lady of the Bayou Homeless Shelter
RSVP: Louise Rivard, cajunhottie@bb.com

"Louise Rivard," she murmured. "That's Tante Lulu. What would Lance have to do with Tante Lulu?"

Her ex-husband was involved in lots of charity events, lending his name to good causes. She was about to pitch this one in the circular file when Patti came into the room. She was all dolled up for a slumber party to be held at her friend Carolyn's tonight.

Good Lord! Are those fishnet stockings she has on under that very short skirt? No, just tights made to look like fishnet. Whew! Patti had long blonde hair, the curls tamed into a series of beaded braids framing her face. Dangly Santa earrings hung from her pierced ears. She had rings on almost all her fingers. On top she wore a black glittery shirt with sequined letters saying, "NASCAR Babe," an ill-thought-out gift for a seven-year-old girl from her Daddy. She had her own unique style, you had to give her that.

"Is that the invitation? Yippee!" Patti squealed, taking the card out of Brenda's hand and dancing around their small kitchen. "Can we go, Mommy? Please. This is a special honor for Daddy, and we hardly ever go to things for Daddy. Please, please, please."

"Oh, I don't know, honey. It's in Louisiana, and—"

"Dad would send us plane tickets."

"And it's a school night."

Patti put both hands on her tiny hips. "It's the Saturday before Christmas, Mom. Does Christmas vacation ring a bell?"

"Don't be smart with me, young lady."

"Sorry." The kid had tears in her eyes, whether for fear that her mother would say no, or the harsh tone, she wasn't sure. "But I wanna be there for Dad. Maybe I could go myself." Her bottom lip quivered, like it always did when she was being brave, but scared silly.

"I am not putting you on a plane by yourself."

Patti looked both relieved and upset.

"How come you know so much about this event? Has your Dad been prompting you to beg me to go?"

"Actually, no. Dad never mentioned it. Probably because you always say no anyhow, no matter what it is, if it involves him."

Am I really that unbending?

"It was Tante Lulu who tol' me 'bout it."

"Huh? Since when do you know Tante Lulu?"

"I met her at the wedding, Mom. Geesh! Dontcha remember?"

"Of course I remember, but I'm surprised that you do." On the other hand, the Cajun lady would be hard to forget.

"She called here one day when you were working down at the Jinx office."

"And you forgot to tell me?"

"I figured you'd say no anyhow. Like you always do."

"That is not true."

"They were scheduling the event and wanted to pick a time when I would be able to attend. See, it's important that I go."

"I would only have a week to diet myself into my Christmas dress," she mused aloud.

"You could buy a new one, in a bigger size."

"Bite your tongue, girl. Wonder if I should try the grapefruit or the sauerkraut diet this time."

It was an indication of how badly Patti wanted to attend that she didn't even groan over the diet fare. "Can I go?" she asked in a small voice.

"Well, if you go, I go."

Brenda was pretty sure she saw a crafty gleam of satisfaction in her daughter's eyes. Had she just been manipulated, Lance Caslow style?

Chapter Three

Can NASCAR drivers shimmy? . . .

Lance was more nervous than he'd ever been at the Daytona when he waited for the loudspeaker to announce, "Gentlemen, start your engines." The jitters never went away. But this was far worse.

"I am not taking my shirt off," he told the LeDeux men backstage as they prepared for the upcoming Cajun Bad Boys show. "NASCAR drivers do not wear jackets without their shirts on. And I for sure am not wearing those tight stripper pants."

"What, you think cops go around bare-chested as they nab bad guys?" John LeDeux wore the bottom half of a police uniform, cop hat on his head at a jaunty angle, and carried a billy club. Lance was one hundred per cent heterosexual, but he had to admit the rogue did look hot.

"And me, do you really think I go into court wearing a suit with no shirt underneath?" Luc LeDeux just grinned at him, looking rakishly handsome in a dark blue pin-striped Boss suit which exposed a black, hairy chest.

René, an environmentalist/teacher, wore only a vest and his *frottoir*, a washboard. He was a part-time musician, playing with the Swamp Rats, which was on stage right now. René was the instigator of these shows. He's the one who encouraged them to do outrageous things, things Lance didn't want to think about.

"Hey, at least they aren't tryin' ta get ya to dance around a fireman's pole," Remy added. He was wearing a bombers jacket, minus a shirt.

"You danced around a fireman's pole?"

"Hell, no, but they tried. Instead I wore dress whites like a freakin' Richard Gere from 'An Officer and a Gentleman.'"

"Holy crap!" he said.

"Actually, they brought out the fireman's pole for an earlier Cajun Bad Boys event. Was it when Sylvie wouldn't talk ta you, Luc?"

"Yep," Luc replied with absolutely no embarrassment.

The two brothers grinned at each other.

"The best thing is that after a performance our women are all turned on," Remy told Lance. "Ain't that right, Luc? There'll be hot times on the bayou tonight."

"Oh, that is just great. Why don'tcha brag when there are single fellas like me around?" This was John speaking.

"Hah! Like you'd have any trouble lining up a bootie call!" Remy said.

These guys were nuts, and not just them. They'd enlisted the help of a New Orleans Saints football player in a helmet, carrying a football, wearing tight, white scrimmage pants, sans underwear and jersey. Then there was The Swamp Cowboy . . . Charmaine's scowling husband, Rusty, who was no more happy to be in this nutcase show than he was. There was also a carpenter with tool belt. And a Richard Simmons lookalike; that was Lance's contribution, to please Tante Lulu. The real Richard told Lance's agent that he would have come, but he had a prior engagement with a half-ton lady in crisis.

Anyhow, this was the LeDeux's crazy, half-assed idea of the Village People. It was a show they put on periodically, which was very popular if the crowd outside, five hundred people strong, paying a hundred dollars a pop, was any indication.

The LeDeux women were no better, dressed in bright colored, thigh-high spandex dresses and stiletto heels, even Tante Lulu.

"I'm going for a walk," he said.

"Don't go too far. We'll be on in a half hour . . . or forty-five minutes," John told him.

"You sure yer comin' back?" Luc inquired.

Good question. He sure didn't feel like it, but then he decided he had to. This was his last shot, and he had to give it his all. "I'll be here," he promised.

Unfortunately, John got the last shot in when he asked him, "Hey, Lance, I sure hope you know how to shimmy."

Sucking it in, physically and mentally . . .

Brenda stood near the entrance of the Cajun Christmas event, sipping at her second glass of white wine.

She could barely breathe, but she wasn't sure if it was because she'd eaten so much food after practically starving herself this past week or if she was afraid to relax for fear of succumbing to Lance's formidable charms. Not that she'd seen the charmer today. Nope, she was avoiding him like a Krispy Kreme donut.

But really, she *was* having a good time. The company was great. All of the LeDeux family had shown up. In fact, there were at least five hundred people here, who had paid one hundred dollars for the charitable cause, just to honor Lance. And to see the LeDeuxs perform, an event not to be missed here on the bayou, she'd been told.

And the food . . . oh, my goodness, the food! On the buffet tables arrayed around the huge banquet room there were Gumbo Ya Ya, red beans and rice, Tipsy Chicken, Jambalaya, gator stew, Crawfish Etouffée, Redfish Court Bouillon, blackened catfish fingers, and Limping Susan, an okra and rice dish, not to mention beaten biscuits dripping with butter. And that was just the entrees. For dessert there were sinfully sweet pralines, bread pudding with whiskey sauce, King Cake, and Tante Lulu's famous Peachy Praline Cobbler Cake. Dieter's heaven, to be sure.

"Sugar, you look hot," Charmaine said, coming up to her.

"Thanks," Brenda said. And she did look hot, as well she should after having spent three hundred dollars on this little red silk slip dress that left her black hose encased legs exposed up to mid-thigh, and her shoulders and chest risking exposure if not for the two thin rhinestone straps. On her feet were red high heels, also with rhinestone straps. Red shoes! A first for Brenda. Her blonde curls had been tamed and upswept, except for a few escaping tendrils. She wore no jewelry except for cheap rhinestone chandelier earrings and the small diamond heart on a gold chain that Lance had given her for a wedding gift eons ago. It was worth practically nothing compared to the more expensive jewelry he'd gifted her over the years, mostly due to guilt. She'd been determined to shine here tonight at her first Lance event in years. "I'm afraid to breathe, or my stomach will pop out."

"I know what you mean." Charmaine laughed. "We've been wearing these spandex dresses for the past five years, and the fabric has to stretch just a little bit more over my hips and butt these days."

Brenda couldn't see where, even with Charmaine being about five months pregnant. All the LeDeux women were going to perform some kind of Motown song and dance number soon, and they were dressed in identical spandex dresses and high heels of different colors. Charmaine filled hers very nicely, thank you very much. She was built like a tall slim beauty queen, which she had been at one time. Miss Louisiana.

Tante Lulu walked up to them then. And, Lordy, Lordy, she was wearing a spandex dress, too. Neon pink with matching pink high heels, though not as high as Charmaine's. And her short curly hair was dyed pink today, too. She looked like a ball of cotton candy. "Didja finish that wine already, Brenda. Lemme go get ya another glass."

"No, no, no," she said, setting her empty wine glass on a nearby empty table. "I'm not much of a drinker, and I'm already feeling a little woozy. I want to be alert for your program."

"Ooooh, I have a good idea," Charmaine cooed. "What we all need is an oyster shooter . . . except mine will have to be minus the booze."

"Charmaine, yer a genius," Tante Lulu concurred. A remarkable statement. "Does ya like oysters, Brenda?"

"Yes, but I've had enough to eat."

"Sweetie, oyster shooters have nothing to do with food."

Leading her to the bar, the two Cajun women asked the bartenders to line up some Oyster shooters. There were Tabasco covered raw oysters in one shot glass and one hundred proof bourbon in the next.

Charmaine leaned her head back, tossed back the oyster, immediately followed by the booze, except hers was non-alcoholic. "Whoo-ee, that's good."

Tante Lulu did the same. No non-alcoholic chaser for her, though. "Thass what I'm talkin' about."

They both turned to her. Brenda was game. She followed suit, and felt the potent drink all the way to her toes. The oyster was spicy. The bourbon was wicked.

Charmaine looked at her, then she and Tante Lulu looked at each other, and grinned.

The two ladies downed another shot and looked at Brenda.

"Oh, I don't think—"

"Thass yer trouble, girlie. Ya think too much." Tante Lulu shoved the two glasses into her hand.

What could she do, except to drink them down.

"How come my lips are numb?" she slurred out then.

"Thass the way it's 'sposed ta be, honey." Tante Lulu patted her shoulder.

Charmaine and Tante Lulu sashayed away then, butts swaying from side to side, leaving Brenda to wonder if she'd just been conned.

Honey, will you blow me . . . dry? . . .

Lance was still walking off his nervousness.

He stopped in a side room in the back hall where a babysitter was watching over some of the kids, including Patti who was playing Barbie dolls with Luc and Remy's little girls. When she saw him, she jumped up and ran over, leaping into his arms. He gave her a hug, twirling her around. "How's it goin', sweetcakes? Havin' fun?"

She leaned her head back. Blonde curls, just like her mother's, were bouncing. "How are *you*, Daddy?"

"Nervous."

Giving him another hug, she said, "Don't be. Tante Lulu showed me how to pray to St. Jude. And he whispered in my ear this morning that everything is gonna be all right."

"St. Jude, huh?" *Now I'm turning my daughter into a fruitcake.*

Hey, I resent that, he thought he heard a voice in his head say. St. Jude? *That is just great. Now, I'm joining the fruitcake club.*

"Have you seen Mom?"

"Nope." He'd been avoiding that confrontation. He didn't want to risk having their usual argument before he even made his grand performance.

"She looks so hot." Patti rolled her eyes meaningfully. "She even bought a new dress. Make sure you tell her how nice it looks, but whatever you do, don't mention diets, fat, weight, or butts."

"Bu . . . butts?" he sputtered.

"Yeah, Mom is really sensitive about the size of her butt these days."

Great! Not only am I taking advice from a woman older than God, but now I'm getting advice from little squirts, too.

That blasted voice in his head said, *Whatever works.*

"See you later, honey."

When he stepped out into the hall, he almost ran into Tante Lulu who was wobbling along on pink high heels that matched her pink stretchy dress. Her hair was dyed pink tonight, too. She looked like an ad for Pepto Bismol.

"Gotta hurry," the old lady told him. "Us girls has gotta decide which Diana Ross songs ta sing. Then mebbe we'll do `Redneck Woman'. Thass by Gretchen Wilson. Hope I remember the words."

"Good luck," he said.

Tante Lulu was already on her way, but she turned and told him, "No, *cher*, good luck to you, but not to worry. Everythin's gonna be okay."

"Is St. Jude talking to you, too?"

"St. Jude allus talks to me. No, I meant that I jist got Brenda ta drink two glasses of wine, and now she's startin' on Oyster Shooters."

"You're getting her drunk? You think her being drunk will help me win her over?" *That's all I need. Brenda too plastered to notice me making a fool out of myself.*

"Not drunk. Jist primin' the pump."

Priming the pump! Good Lord! That's something one of my pit crew would say.

He must have looked dubious because she continued, "You know what they say. 'Wine makes good women wenches.' Well, here in the south we say, 'Oyster Shooters make wild women wilder'."

"Brenda . . . a wild wench?" he muttered to Tante Lulu's back. "I am in deep shit." He went into a side corridor, used by employees, and leaned against the wall, putting both hands to his face. Of course, it was just his luck that Brenda walked out of the ladies room just then. Rather, she staggered out of the ladies room.

"I had ta pee, and the other line was too long," she explained, as if he needed an explanation for her coming out of an employees' bathroom. "My tongue is so thick. Look at it. Does it look thick ta you."

To his amazement, Brenda came right up to him—within touching distance, for the love of Dale Earnhardt!—and stuck her tongue out real far. He could practically see her tonsils.

"Looks fine to me," he said, but what he really wanted to say was, "I don't know, darling, maybe you better stick it in my mouth so I can make sure."

"Whatja doin' out here? Shouldn't the guest of honor be . . . guest of honoring?" She giggled at her own lame joke.

"I came down this corridor 'cause I'm a little nervous."

She cocked her head to the side . . . and almost fell over. "You never get nervous in public. Never, ever, never."

"I am now."

It was then he took in her outfit. "Holy crap, Brendie! You are one freakin' hottie tonight. Wow!" She was wearing this short, red, hardly-there dress, which couldn't possibly have a bra under it. Her long legs were covered with sheer black stockings. Man, he loved her legs. He especially loved her legs in black stockings. She wore red stiletto heels to match her dress, thus raising her up to his height, which was kind of nice. And her lips were covered with red, screw-me-quick lip gloss.

"Wow! back at you," she said before he could test the screw-me-quick lip gloss.

"You think I look good?" Compliments from Brenda were a rarity. In fact, they'd been non-existent for the past five years.

"You always look good."

She stood swaying before him.

He stood biting his bottom lip with nervousness.

"Are you all right?" they both said at the same time.

Deciding that he didn't want to risk some employee—or worse yet a member of the press sneaking in through the kitchen—finding Brenda in this condition, he steered her toward what turned out to be an employees lounge. Once inside, he locked the door, and hoped there would be a vending machine here . . . with black coffee. There wasn't.

But Brenda solved her own problem. She laid down on the chaise, then stretched her arms over her head.

Which caused her short dress to become even shorter.

Which caused the half-hard-on he always had around her to go full tilt boogie.

He now knew that she wore only panty hose, no panties.

"Why don't you stay there, honey, and I'll go get you some coffee."

"Doan want no coffee."

"What do you want?"

"You."

Oh. My. God. The answer to all my dreams, and she has to be drunk. This is not funny, St. Jude. Not funny at all.

I think it is, that blasted voice in his head said. *We call it celestial humor.*

"You don't mean that, Brendie. You've been drinking?" *That was a dumb thing to say. As if she didn't already know she'd been drinking.*

"No, I've been eating," she disagreed. "Oysters. Oyster Shooters."

"Don't they have straight bourbon in them?"

"Whass yer point? Oysters are an affer . . . apro . . . aphro-dis-iac, ya know? Whoo-boy, are they ever! I feel like I've swallowed a bucketload of Viagra."

Information I do not need in my condition. Maybe later, but not now. Not now when I have to go on a stage pretty damn soon and make a fool out of myself. She scooted herself over toward the wall, making a little bit of room on the chaise. She crooked her finger at him and said, "Wanna make out?"

He smiled.

"I hate it when you do that?" She licked her lips, a slow sexy procedure that made him wonder, if only for a blip of a second, if it would really be morally wrong to make love to Brenda when she was crocked. "My lips are numb. Mebbe . . . *maybe* there was sugarcane, I mean, Novocain in those drinks."

"You hate it when I do what, honey?"

"Smile. It makes me get butterflies here." She placed both hands over her tummy.

Lance noticed something then. A small diamond heart on a chain. He'd given it to Brenda on their wedding night. Was her wearing it a sign of something important . . . a change in her attitude toward him? Was the liquor just bringing out in the open her real feelings? Had she finally, *finally*, forgiven him? *Please, God,* he prayed. *Please, St. Jude.*

I'm here, I'm here, the voice in his head said.

Was it God or St. Jude or his subconscious? Hell, maybe it was bleepin' Santa Claus. *Whatever!*

His better judgment told him to be a good boy, that if he lay down with Brenda, she would hate him later.

But his not-so-good judgment just laughed.

So, he eased himself down onto the foot or so of space she'd made for him, pulled her into his embrace, then kissed the top of her curly head. An indication of her inebriation was the fact that she didn't shove him off the couch, onto his ass. Instead, she cuddled up against him. It was the closest they'd been in such a long time that Lance's heart constricted in his chest walls.

"I feel like havin' sex," she said all of a sudden.

His you-know-what lurched. He was afraid to breathe.

Lance was stunned.

"But maybe we could just kiss a little," she added.

Not a good idea. Definitely not! he thought even as he lowered his head and pressed his mouth against hers.

They both moaned.

It had been so long, and he and Brenda knew how to kiss each other. They'd been doing it for almost thirty years, since they were both five years old and worried that she might get preggers from kissing. In fact, he and Brenda could bring each other to climax, just by kissing. And if she kept it up . . . licking the roof of his mouth . . . that's just what was going to happen.

They were both panting when he forcibly took Brenda's face in both his hands and held her away from him. Her lips were kiss swollen and minus the sexy red lipstick, which he assumed he wore now.

Brenda stared at him, her blue eyes dazed.

He was in a daze, too. Otherwise, he would have been prepared for her leg being thrown over his, and her sitting up, all in one move, which was remarkable considering her condition. But, whoa, she was straddling him now, her dress hiked up to her waist.

He had a hard-on that could drill concrete, and it was planted smack dab inside her cleft, just where she liked to be touched. The fabric of her panty hose, and the fabric of his pants didn't buffer the sensation much at all. She rocked against him, just to let him know she was there . . . in case he hadn't noticed. Hah!

"My nipples are hard," she said.

"I noticed," he choked out.

"They ache."

He leaned upward.

She leaned downward.

And he took one nipple into his mouth right through her silk dress and began to suckle her with the hard rhythm he knew she liked.

She screamed. She actually screamed. And began to buck against his erection.

He moved to her other breast.

She was one continuous wail as she came and came and came against him.

Then she just folded like a rag doll, placed her face against his racing heart, and fell asleep.

He would have laughed if he weren't so blistering hot and turned on. While she'd been coming apart, he still hadn't got his rocks off.

But then his cell phone rang. He managed to pull it out of his pocket without disturbing Brenda, who was snoring softly now into his ear. "Yeah?" he barked into the phone.

"Where the hell are you?" John asked him. "We're ready to go on."

"Uh . . . I'm in kind of an awkward situation here."

"You aren't going to bail on us, are you?"

"I'm not sure."

John was swearing a blue streak and someone grabbed the phone from him. Tante Lulu. Great! That's just what he needed.

"Get yet butt out here, boy. No time ta get shy now. There's five hundred people, jist waitin' ta see yer purty face. I'll give ya five minutes, boy."

He was about to explain why he couldn't make it, especially not that fast, but there was a dial tone now.

It took him at least five minutes just to wake Brenda up. It took another five minutes for him to drag her into the bathroom and put wet towels on her face, trying to sober her up.

Once she was half-sober, she looked in the mirror and squealed. "Aaarrgh! What did you do to me?"

"Hey! It's more a case of what you did to me," he replied using the wet paper towel to wipe the lipstick off his face. "Frankly, sweetheart, I think you look real good."

Her hairdo had come undone. She wore no lipstick, but she did sport lips that some Botox junkies would envy. And there were two wet spots in strategic places on her dress.

She tried to punch him and missed.

He laughed.

She hissed. "Help me,' she demanded. "I can't go back out there like this."

So it was that when his cell phone rang again, fifteen minutes later—he'd ignored the last ten calls—he picked it up and heard a crowd chanting, "Caslow, Caslow, Caslow!"

"Do you hear that, you worthless loser?" Charmaine snarled. "That's your fans about to storm the stage."

"I'll be there as soon as I can."

"Why can't you come now?"

Lance had had enough of the badgering. "If you must know, I'm blow drying Brenda's boobs."

There was a stunned silence, followed by laughter.

"And Tante Lulu thought you needed love advice!"

The things a guy will do for love . . .

Brenda, now stone cold sober, sat sipping black coffee at a table near the stage. Her daughter Patti and the two LeDeux girls sat with her. The other chairs at their table were empty for the moment because the LeDeuxs were about to present their Cajun Bad Boys show.

She was counting the minutes till she could escape back to her hotel room and hide her head under a pillow, pretending she hadn't made the biggest fool of herself. Five years of hiding her feelings down the drain!

Lance was nowhere to be seen. Good thing, too. She would probably wallop him a good one for taking advantage of her.

No, that wasn't true. She was the one who'd gotten herself drunk and put the moves on him. Her face heated up at the image of the two of them on the chaise. And her climaxing, while he did not. Pathetic, that's what she was.

Let's face it, she told herself, *I still love the man. Never stopped. The booze just loosened my will to hide it.*

"It's starting, Mommy." Patti reached over and squeezed her hand. Her daughter sensed her inner turmoil. Not for the first time, she saw that her little girl was way too mature for her age.

The canned music that had been playing stopped, and Tante Lulu wobbled out to center stage and pulled the microphone down to meet her height. "First off, lemme thank y'all fer comin' ta support the homeless hereabouts. Since Hurricane Katrina . . . well, y'all know how bad off some folks are, even after all these years. Ta show our thanks, we gots some top notch entertainment fer ya."

The band began to play softly at first while Tante Lulu went on, "Ever'one knows that love is what makes the world go 'round, and iffen ya doan know that, then yer jist dumbclucks."

A titter of laughter went through the crowd. Tante Lulu was known to most of the people here.

"Well, thass what we're here ta celebrate tonight. Love. And Cajuns, of course."

Tante Lulu stepped back, the lights dimmed, except for a spotlight, the music got louder, recognizable now as that old Supremes song "Stop! In the Name of Love." Dancing out in a snakelike fashion were Charmaine, well-known to this crowd because of her chain of beauty salons; Sylvie LeDeux, a chemist and Luc's wife; Rachel LeDeux, a Feng Shui decorator and Remy's wife; and Valerie LeDeux, a lawyer and wife to René, an environmentalist, teacher, musician, and allegedly the biggest rascal in the world. They wore very short spandex dresses in bright colors with matching stiletto heels. They sang. They danced. They laughed and got the audience laughing, too. In fact, the audience stood, clapping and singing along when Tante Lulu joined the girls in a rousing rendition of Aretha Franklin's "R. E. S. P. E. C. T."

"Hey, ladies," a male voice came through the speakers, overriding the tail end of their song. "That respect goes both ways." It sounded like the slow Southern drawl of René, but it could have been any one of the Cajun gentlemen.

"Oh, yeah?" Charmaine said, putting her hands on her hips. The other ladies did the same.

"Do ya'll think ya could do better?" Tante Lulu chirped in.

"*Mais, oui, chère.*"

The ladies stepped to the side and the band launched into a rowdy version of the Village People's "Macho Man," except they were singing different lyrics with the words changed to "Cajun Man." They shimmied out onto the stage, strutting, winking at the crowd, letting out an occasional Rebel yell, singing and dancing in the expert, enthusiastic way only Cajun men could. And their attire! Luc in a day-old beard wore a business suit sans shirt and looked sexier than if he wore nothing at all. Remy wore a bomber jacket, Aviator sunglasses and also had no shirt on. René, the most outrageous, wore a vest and no shirt, carried a *frottir*, a Cajun washboard instrument, and unbuttoned jeans that rode low on his hips. His wife, the lawyer, gaped at his attire. Rusty Lanier, Charmaine's husband, clearly unhappy to be there, wore his usual cowboy attire . . . hat, boots with spurs, tight jeans and no shirt. He looked at Charmaine as if he'd like to kill her; she looked as if she'd like to do something entirely different to him. Last came the youngest LeDeux, John or Tee-John. He was a cop, with unbuttoned shirt, cop hat and billy club. The most uninhibited of the bunch, he was the best dancer, with sexy moves, and he teased the crowd by continually shrugging his shirt off his shoulders like a stripper.

There were others, as well. Some athletes, a fire fighter, and the most godawful Richard Simmons impersonator.

After their rendition of "Cajun Man" they segued into their version of "In the Navy," except of course they made it "In the Bayou." Some of the lyrics were more than suggestive.

At one point, René pulled his resisting wife back onto center stage with him and made her dance with him, a sensual kind of dirty dance where he spooned her from behind. She was embarrassed, at first, but then got into the dance, too. They were good together.

Brenda was really enjoying herself, and so was everyone else. No wonder people paid a hundred dollars for this charity event. The show was worth that and much more.

Her heart constricted, though, to see these Cajun men and their wives together. They clearly loved each other, and had fun together. Mismatched, and still able to keep their marriages together.

Unlike her and Lance.

Which made her wonder . . . where was he? After all, this event was supposed to be about him.

But then . . . oh, my goodness! . . . then she found out exactly where he was.

"VAROOM! VAROOM! VAROOM!" The sound of a loud racing motor was heard before the car moved onto the stage, and everyone moved to the side. It was the car Lance had driven in his first Indy win eight years ago.

The crowd went wild. Standing, clapping, screaming out his name even before Lance flipped the switch that caused the roof to rise. Then he stepped out.

He wore black slacks, low heeled boots, his NASCAR jacket with all the sponsor badges, as well as some of his winning commemoratives. His face was lowered and hidden by dark sunglasses and a NASCAR baseball cap.

But then the music started to play again . . . the "Macho Man" melody, but now the lyrics were "NASCAR Man." He raised his head, took off his sunglasses and seemed to look right at her. He was unsmiling and serious. Little alarm bells began to go off in her head. She'd heard stories about some of these Cajun Bad Boy events, which she'd disregarded . . . till now. Something about their whole purpose being some Tante Lulu matchmaking exercise.

"This is for you, babe." He pointed a finger her way, and a spotlight was suddenly on her. "But if I'm gonna make a fool of myself, you are, too." Two security men appeared at her side. Then, mimicking the NASCAR phrase, "Gentlemen, start your engines," he said, "Gentlemen, start her engine."

With great fanfare, she was escorted to the stage, where Lance put an arm around her shoulder and tucked her into his side. She muttered under her breath, "I'm gonna kill you." To which he replied, also in an undertone, "You've been killing me for the past five years. What else is new?"

"Since this whole show tonight is about love, according to Tante Lulu, let me tell you a little story," Lance said into the mike. "I have loved this woman here," he kissed the top of her head, "for thirty years. How is that possible, you ask, since I'm thirty-five? Well, Brendie and I have known each other since we were practically toddlers. I think I fell in love with her the day her diaper drooped and I got my first gander at her very fine behind."

She snorted her opinion, and leaned into the microphone. "That is a lie. He fell in love with me when I let him win our first tricycle race."

He squeezed her shoulders. "That, too."

"Then how come you're divorced?" a male in the back of the room shouted out.

"Good question. You want to take that one, or should I, Brendie?"

"Oh, by all means, you take it, *Lancie*. This is your show." Then she put her face in her free hand, wondering how to extricate herself from this situation.

"I screwed up. For a blip of a second, I forgot what was important. And I've been trying ever since then to make it up. I love her, never stopped." He tipped her chin up so she would look at him and said in a softer voice, "I love you."

"How 'bout you, Brenda. Do you love him?" It was someone behind them on the stage asking that question. Possibly Charmaine.

Brenda was going to refuse to answer that question, but then she noticed Patti staring up at her with such hope in her eyes. "I never stopped loving him, but—" She put up a halting hand before anyone got the wrong impression, "I've learned that love is not enough."

"Says who?" a woman in audience yelled out.

"Okay, baby, here's the deal," Lance said, turning her with a hand on each shoulder so she faced him. "I can get down on one knee and ask you to marry me, again, or—" He waggled his eyebrows at her.

"Or . . . " He unzipped his jacket, down, then back up again, letting her know he wore nothing under the jacket.

"Or what?"

"Or this." He motioned to the back of the stage, and a chair was brought up. He pushed her down in the chair, gave a signal for the music to begin again, then began to dance for her. A slow, seductive, teasing strip tease that began with the removal of his jacket, then the unbuckling and tossing of his belt, the undoing of the button at his waist and the beginning of an unzip. She saw bare skin behind the zipper.

She stood suddenly, unable to let this go any farther. Lance didn't like to dance, and he didn't do it very well. He hated even more humbling himself publicly. The fact that he was doing it told her something important. She wasn't sure what, but she couldn't let him continue.

Taking the microphone from him, she told the crowd, "Stay tuned, folks. Lance and I have got to go have a little chat." She winked at them meaningfully. "Maybe I have an early Christmas gift for him."

Then she took Lance's hand and said in a low voice, "Zip up, soldier. What I have to say requires total concentration, and I can't do it with your navel blinking at me."

He laughed and followed her willingly.

Behind them, the band began to play and the entertainment continued, without them.

Neither of them said anything. He was probably afraid of what she would say.

She could tell that he was surprised when she took him to the same employees' lounge where they had been before.

And he was even more surprised when she locked the door.

The miracle was . . .

Lance stood with his back against the door, silent. This was it, he knew it was. Brenda was about to ring the death knell on their marriage. There was no hope.

But, whoa, Brenda was reaching behind to unzip her dress. When she turned, her dress slid down to the floor at her feet in a puddle of red silk. She wore only panty hose and red high heels. And the diamond heart pendant he'd given her on their wedding night light years ago. Leaning forward, giving him a spectacular view of her hanging breasts, she removed her panty hose. Then she put the high heels back on again.

"Brendie, what are you doing?" It was amazing he could even ask the question with the erotic buzz ringing in his ears, his heart racing like a souped up engine, and his cylinder about to take off.

"Finishing what you started," she said.

At first he thought she meant that she wanted to finish making love, but then she pulled a hard backed chair to the middle of the floor, sat down and crossed her legs. "Well, big boy, show me what you can do." With a wave of her hand she indicated his half-unzipped pants.

"You know I can't dance worth spit."

"Oh, I think you were doing very well."

"Yeah?" He grinned and listened for the beat of the music they could hear in the distant banquet room. He did in fact dance for her, stripping one item of clothing at a time. When he was as naked as she was, and she'd made various remarks about his anatomy, all complimentary, he was about to pull her to her feet, but instead, he went down on one knee, and said, "Brenda, will you marry me, again?" He didn't want this to be just about sex.

"Of course."

"Whaaaat? What do you mean, *of course?*"

"Just that, honey."

He pulled her up and put his arms around her. Once he had kissed her till she was as breathless as he was, he asked, "When did you decide this?"

"Probably five years ago, when I left, but I had to give you time—"

"Give me time?" he barked. "More like give you time to punish me."

"Exactly."

"But when did you decide I'd been punished enough?"

"At the A & P. When I discovered that you'd bought all the

tabloids."

"You liked that, huh?"

She nodded. "I did."

After they made love . . . really made love . . . on the chaise, twice, he cuddled her against him, and asked, "When can we get remarried?"

"I was thinking Christmas Eve. It's the only present Patti has been asking for."

"Sounds good to me."

As they dressed and prepared to go out to tell Patti and the others their news, Lance couldn't help but ponder how hopeless he'd felt these past weeks . . . till he'd gone to Tante Lulu for help. And he wondered if maybe, just maybe, the old lady did know something the rest of them didn't.

As they left the room, hand in hand, he felt something in his jacket pocket press against his side. He knew exactly what it was. The St. Jude statue Tante Lulu had given him.

He began to ask Brenda, "Do you believe in—"

"—St. Jude?" she finished for him. "I was just thinking the same thing."

In that instant, they both realized that they'd experienced their own form of Christmas miracle.

"I love you, Brendie."

"I love you, Lance."

And the voice in both their heads said, "Another job done!" Or maybe it was "Ho, ho, ho!"

Continue reading for more information about Sandra Hill's books and an excerpt from 'Twas the Night

'Twas the Night

More Romantic Christmas Fun!
From Sandra Hill, Kate Holmes and Trish Jensen

Excerpt

Tuesday, evening, three days 'til Christmas Eve.

"Gotcha!"

With that single word, when her attention had wandered for all of a nanosecond, Sam cornered her in the back of the bus by sliding onto the bench seat next to her, thus trapping her against the window. What a tight squeeze it was, too, considering her bulk in the Santa suit!

"You are so juvenile," she said with a sniff.

"Yep," he agreed and adjusted his body closer to hers, something she would not have thought possible.

With all the movement he was making, he shook some of the boxes stacked behind. There was a chorus of "Suzie Gotta Pee," "Suzie Gotta Pee," "Suzie Gotta Pee," "Suzie Gotta Pee" from some of the gifts left over from the last shelter stop.

"What the hell?" Sam exclaimed as he turned to straighten the talking boxes.

"Samuel Merrick!" Emma Smith chided from the seat in front of them. Emma, a large, husky woman, much like Camryn Manheim, but older, and brusquer, was a retired eighth grade teacher, who had taught them all. The one thing she could not abide was bad language and she heard every bit of it with her trusty Miracle-Ear hearing aid. "Tsk, tsk, tsk!"

Sam folded his hands in his lap and said, "Sorry, ma'am," batting his eyelashes with exaggeration. Once Emma turned around with a huff, he ruined the good little boy effect by winking at Reba. God, that wink went through her like an erotic current. The man was lethal. And way too close.

She doubted whether pushing him would do much good; the determined gleam in his eyes said loud and clear that no quarter would be given by this soldier, not after her having blocked all his previous moves. Plus, he had about seventy-five pounds on her. She supposed she could scream for help, but what a sight that would be . . . nine overaged Santas to the rescue . . . assuming they would come to her rescue, considering how Sam was charming the liver spots off of them all . . . darn it.

Yep, Sam had her right where he wanted her, apparently, after a day and some odd hours of the pursuit-and-avoid game they'd been playing. *Who am I kidding? It's exactly twenty-eight hours and thirty-five minutes since The Good-bye Kiss . . . not that I'm keeping tabs. And, heavens to Betsy, why am I feeling all melty inside at the prospect of the louse's having me where he wants me?*

"Hello," Sam said.

"Good-bye," she said.

He smiled.

She frowned.

He took her hand in his.

She pulled her hand away from his.

It was all so childish. But they weren't children anymore, and Reba couldn't risk the powerful wave of pain that would surely accompany any association with Sam. She didn't want to hear his phony excuses. She didn't want to discuss her long-standing anger toward him. She didn't want anything to do with the testosterone-oozing hunk. Stiffening her spine, she steeled herself to resist the allure he offered, and, yes, he was alluring, even as he merely sat beside her. Seemingly innocent. Never innocent.

He reached for her hand again, and she swatted him away, again, but harder this time. "Ouch," he said with a grin.

"Cut it out, Sam. Just cut it out."

The fury underlying her words must have struck a chord in him somewhere. He stilled. "What?"

"Don't touch me. Don't talk to me. In fact, don't even look at me. Don't think I haven't noticed the way you watch me all the time, just waiting for a chance to pounce."

"Hey, I do not pounce." He studied her carefully as if trying to figure out some puzzle. Then, he concluded in typical Dumb Man fashion, "You are being really intense here, sweetheart. That has got to be a good sign. If you didn't care, you wouldn't react so strongly, right?

You must not want me near you because you fear the temptation. Yep, a very good sign."

"Either that, or you repulse me."

He appeared to give that serious consideration, then decided, "No, no, no! I won't consider that possibility."

"Stay away from me, Sam. I'm not one of your groupies. I'm not your . . . anything."

The vehemence of her response seemed to stun him, but then he immediately switched to irritation. "Groupies? Are you nuts? I have never been into the Blues' groupie scene."

"I wasn't talking about the Blue Angels. I was talking about you, Mister Egomaniac."

"Me? You are suffering from a huge misconception, honey. I don't have groupies."

"Oh, Sam, you've always had groupies."

He threw his hands in the air. "This is a ridiculous conversation. I don't want to talk about me. I want to talk about you. I want to talk about us."

"Here's a news flash. There is no us."

The sadness on his face tore at her soul, but at least he had the good judgment to say nothing for a few moments. He must have sensed her growing agitation and realized that the best thing he could do was sit silently next to her and let her grow accustomed to his presence. Which she would never do. Not now. Not ever. No way. Please, God!

When did it turn so warm in here? Betty must have jacked up the heat.

When did Sam start wearing aftershave, or was that tangy evergreen scent just a residue of soap on his skin? Heck it was probably just the greenery that decorated each of the windows in the bus. How pathetic was she?

When would she stop noticing every little thing about him? The intriguing laugh lines that bracketed the edges of his blue eyes and the corners of his firm mouth. Or perhaps they were sun crinkles, living in Florida as he did much of the year. Then, there was his rigid military demeanor, even when he stretched his long legs out into the aisle, or joked with the senior Santas, or, Saints forbid, gazed at her with a longing that was anything but soldierly. And, criminey, he had a body perfectly honed to suit the military and a grown woman's humming hormones.

She must have been more exhausted than she'd realized to have allowed Sam to slip past her watchful guard. It was only eight p.m. But she'd been up since five. In the midst of some stress over the weather conditions, they'd performed two shows today, in Sarasota Springs, New York, and Burlington, Vermont, after which they'd picked up Stan and his lady friend, Dana . . . rather, George's friend, Dana . . . or was it both? In any case, she was on the way to the wedding, too. That, on top of JD and the Amish woman, Callie, hopping onto the bus this morning. They were becoming a regular reunion commune. Right now, JD and Callie were sitting on the front seat of the bus, with Stan and Dana on the opposite side. The two men were chatting amiably across the aisle, while the women stared pensively out the darkened windows.

"That was not a good-bye kiss. No way was that a good-bye kiss!" Sam declared, out of the blue, jarring her out of her mental wanderings. Good Lord, the man was resuming a day-old conversation, as if it had never been interrupted.

"I am not going to discuss this."

"This?"

"Us," she said. "It's over . . . done with."

"No, it's not, Reba. God, I hate that song. I can't think when I hear that song. Can't you make them stop?"

"Huh?" Reba glanced up, realizing that her Santa crew had started caroling, as they often did, not just to practice for their homeless shelter events, but because they were, frankly, a cheerful group. It was the holiday season, for goodness sake. "What do you have against Christmas songs, Mr. Grinch?"

He poked her playfully in the arm, but the playfulness never reached his somber eyes. "I don't hate all Christmas songs, just that one," he grumbled.

She narrowed her eyes at him, interested, despite herself. "And why would that be? Too lower class for a hoity-toity celebrity pilot?"

At first, it appeared as if he wouldn't answer her, but then he disclosed something he hadn't shared with her in all the eight years she'd known him.

"My mother gave me up two days before Christmas when I was ten years old. Just walked into a police station, said she needed to find a home for me, plopped down a paltry little cardboard box with all my worldly belongings, and left. Just like that. In the background, that stinkin' 'Jingle Bells' song was playing. I'll never forget it. Me screaming like a banshee for my mother to come back, and Bing Crosby crooning away with those cheerful cornball lyrics."

Suddenly, a look of horror spread over his face as he realized how much he'd revealed. "Forget I said that. God above! Here I am trying to charm you into talking with me. Instead, you must think I'm downright pitiful."

Reba didn't think he was pitiful, at all. In fact, she was deeply touched. "You've certainly come a long way since then, Sam. Your mother would be so proud of you."

"My mother could have cared less."

Reba would have liked to argue that point. After all, she held a masters degree in psychology. Here was a man with major unresolved issues . . . and not just dealing with his mother. But it was none of her business, really.

He ran the fingertips of one hand over his forehead, an unconscious effort to smooth out the creases.

Reba had to make a fist to keep herself from reaching out and doing the smoothing herself.

"Tell me about The Santa Brigade . . . and Winter Haven. I never thought you'd follow in your Dad's footsteps with a nursing home."

"It just happened. I was in private practice . . . working for a Bangor psychological clinic when Dad got cancer. I took a leave to come home and care for him, which meant taking over directorship of the retirement community on a temporary basis. It hasn't been a nursing home for years, by the way. Dad was in hospice for a year before he died. By then I discovered that I liked the work, and I took over." She shrugged. What she left out was the agony of that year, caring for a loved one through that horrendous disease.

"It appears as if you've made the retirement community your own, though. Lots of modern ideas."

She tilted her head in question. "Oh, you mean The Santa Brigade?"

"That and the mandatory volunteer program and physical fitness regime you instituted. Maudeen told me about them while I was showing her how to reorganize some of her files this afternoon."

"You're a computer expert, too?"

He laughed. "Not quite a computer geek. Jets are all high tech today, though, and pilots are required to have advanced computer training."

"You? The person who took algebra twice?"

"Hey, I just wanted to be with you. I liked the way you tutored me." Reba had been a year younger than Sam, thus taking the same courses the year following him. She chose to ignore the eyebrow jiggling trick that accompanied his latter statement.

Now would be a good time to change the subject. "How about you? Do you intend to make the military a career?"

"If you'd asked me that a year ago, I probably would have said I'm destined to be a lifer. But I'm not sure now. At the least, this is my third and last year with the Blues. It's a policy to rotate squadron members every few years on a staggered basis, so there are always familiar faces. The Blues have never been a permanent career option. At the same time, I'm feeling burned out with the Navy these days. I've already served four tours in Iraq and Afghanistan, which is enough, but I have no idea what else I could do . . . in civilian life."

My goodness, Sam was opening up a lot today. He always used to keep his personal doubts inside, as if they signified weakness. It was probably a ploy, though she didn't think he'd go that far. "You could do anything you wanted, Sam."

"I don't know about that. I wish you could have seen me perform with the Blues, though, Reba. I'm a screw-up in lots of ways, but I'm a really good pilot. Hot damn, but I would have showed off for you."

"You always showed off for me, Sam. Whether it was skiing down Suicide Run, or diving off the high board." She shouldn't tell him, she really shouldn't. Oh, heck! "Actually, I did see you, Sam."

"You did? As a Blue Angel? When?"

"Two years ago, in Boston. You . . . the team . . . were great."

He took her hand in his and held tight this time. "You came to a Blue Angels show, and never contacted me? Why not?"

"What was the point?"

"The point? I'll tell you the point," he said hotly, squeezing her hand painfully. "We were friends. Good friends. Whatever else we might have been, friendship demands common courtesy. I can't believe you were so close and didn't even talk to me."

"I intended to, but there were lots of people surrounding you after the show."

"And you couldn't wait? Or yell out my name to get my attention?"

"There were girls there, Sam, and women. I wasn't about to become one of your groupies."

"Groupies again?" he muttered.

"What did you say?"

"Nothing, babe. Nothing."

"And stop calling me babe and honey and sweetheart."

He grinned, as if—yep—he was getting to her.

He was, but that was irrelevant.

"Are you involved with anyone? A relationship, I mean?" Another of those disarming, out-of-the-blue questions.

"No. Nothing steady."

"Good."

Good? What did that mean? It was not good with regard to him. Whether she had a boyfriend, or lover, shouldn't concern him in any way.

"And you?" she asked. Jeesh! Her brain must be splintering apart to be continuing this line of conversation.

He shook his head.

And she thought, "good."

"I've had lots of women —"

"No kidding."

"Would you let me finish, Ms. Smart-ass? I've had lots of women . . . well, not lots . . . but enough."

She barely restrained a sarcastic remark.

"But none of them ever lasted more than a few months. I never even lived with a woman. I certainly never loved any of them . . . not like I . . ."

He let his words trail off, and Reba just knew that the reason was because he wasn't sure what tense to use. Was it "not like I loved you?" Or "not like I love you?"

Not that it mattered.

"I told you that I wasn't going to discuss this, and I meant it." She stood up abruptly and yanked her hand out of his. "Golly, it's hot in here. Move, so I can take off my blasted Santa suit." Enough of hiding behind this disguise. If she didn't cool down soon, she was going to have a stroke, or something. Probably a hormone meltdown.

Sam stared at Reba for several long moments. He was about to resist her order, but then, a good soldier knew how to pick his battles.

"Act calm. Be in control. Never show emotion," he murmured the mantra under his breath.

He'd made some progress with Reba tonight. Best he step back and let her assimilate everything that had been said and the emotions that still sizzled between them. "Okay," he said. "I'll stop . . . for now. But I'm not going away, Reba. We have things that need to be cleared up."

"Like what, Sam?"

"Like why I never came back? Like why you got married? Like where we go from here?"

Before she had a chance to make some wiseacre comment about there being a snowball's chance in hell that they were going anywhere together, he stood up next to her, gave her a quick peck on the mouth before she had a chance to belt him a good one, then moved to the half-empty bench seat across the aisle. The window side of the seat was piled high with boxes of candy canes. All around him he heard people speaking in the deep Maine burr that was at once familiar, and oddly soothing to him.

Reba was already peeling off the Santa suit, as if it were on fire. He felt a little hot himself, but his body heat emanated from an entirely different source. Hey, maybe Reba's heat was the same as his. Hmmmm. How to capitalize on that?

"Would you like a little refreshment?" an elderly voice asked him. Actually, the offer was made by two elderly voices. One held a tray filled with paper cups of egg nog, and the other a tray of sliced fruitcake. It was the spinster twins, Maggie and Meg MacClaren. Their matching, perfectly coifed pinkish blond hairdos never seemed to lose their old-fashioned deep waves. They reminded everyone of those two elderly Baldwin sisters on *The Waltons.*

Since neither fruitcake or eggnog were his personal favorite, and besides, they'd just eaten dinner, if it could be called that, at the homeless shelter in Burlington, he shook his head, hard.

"That was a great show you ladies put on today."

Both sisters beamed.

"Well, thank you, Sam. I was most pleased by the reception Sister and I got for our reading of *A Christmas Carol.* I swear I saw a tear in the eye of that incorrigible lad . . . the one with orange spiked hair," Maggie said in her refined, soft-spoken voice. She leaned down and pressed her parchment-like skin next to his for a quick air-kiss.

Maggie and Meg were about five-foot tall, and tiny . . . and smart as whips. At their advanced age, they were better known to the general public as Dr. Maggie and Dr. Meg. Former Harvard professors of anthropology, they had developed a reputation late in life with their outrageous non-fiction books related to sex and aging . . . sort of a combination Dr. Ruth Westheimer and Margaret Mead. Although retired from teaching and the talk show circuits, they were still amazingly active. In fact, their most recent effort, *Super Sex After Seventy*, hit the NYT list for several weeks last year. The year before they had a runaway bestseller with, *Viagra: Why Is Grandma Smiling?*

"Would you like a little advice?" Dr. Meg offered then.

"About sex?" he choked out.

Reba, who was tossing pillows into a storage bin behind her seat, made a choking sound as well.

"No, dear, not about sex," Dr. Meg said with a soft laugh. "About love." But then, she quickly added, "Unless you need advice about sex."

"I could recommend a book," Dr. Maggie offered.

"Uh, I think I'll pass for now," he said, well aware that his face was flaming. "Maybe later."

"Maybe later," Reba scoffed, once the sisters moved back up the aisle, offering their refreshments to others on the bus.

He was about to tell Reba to be careful, or he would sic the elderly sex experts on her, but the words died in his throat.

Because now—*Holy hell, now*—Reba in a black turtleneck and a pair of tight black jeans was in the aisle, bent over at the waist, tying a pair of athletic shoes.

There were some things a woman should never do in front of a full-blooded male. At the top of the list was bending over in tight black jeans.

He wouldn't even bother trying to resist the temptation. Nosiree! He snaked a hand out and pinched her on the ass.

"Eeekkk!" Reba shrieked, jerking upright and pivoting on her heels to confront her attacker. "You jerk! I could have had a heart attack, you scared me so bad."

"Not to worry, sweetheart, I'm a certified EMT. You oughta see my killer technique for cardiovascular resuscitation?"

"Mouth to mouth, no doubt," she said as she rubbed her butt.

And a very nice butt it was, he noted, then frowned. "Hey, you look different. Have you lost weight?"

She grunted her disgust.

"Bend over again so I can check it out."

She had to laugh at that. "Not in this lifetime."

"It's good to see you smile again, Reba. Did you know, you haven't smiled at me once, since you saw me yesterday? I've missed your smile. I've missed you."

She straightened, giving him his first full view of the new Reba. She had lost weight, and she was in good physical condition. Really good. Talk about eye candy!

"Don't you dare stare at me like that." She practically hissed.

He tried, but could not suppress a grin. "How?"

"Like . . . like you really, really want me."

"Oh, baby, was that ever in doubt?"

*

"Do you do tricks?"

Sam choked on his coffee as the I'm-so-straitlaced-I-could-be-a-saint Emma Smith, who must be close to seventy years old, voiced her outrageous question. And she was looking straight at him. All six-foot, two hundred pounds of her.

He felt as if he were back in her class, and she'd just asked him what he was doing with that notebook in his lap.

"Why me?" He waved a hand to indicate Stan, who sat next to him, on the outside, and JD who sat across from him in the booth. They were indulging in catch-up conversation over cups of coffee in "Grease," the diner located next door to the Sleepytime Motel, where they would sleep that night. Some of the Santa Brigade members had gone off to their rooms, including Reba, while others still straggled behind, sitting in booths in front and behind them, and across the aisle. They were critiquing their latest shelter performances over tea, decaffeinated coffee and prune juice. With respect to that latter beverage, the one thing that Sam had learned while on the Santa bus was that the regular functioning of "plumbing" was of extreme importance to the elderly. They did not hesitate to talk about it, publicly, and give unsolicited advice to him or anyone else within their radar.

But that was neither here nor there. He was more concerned about JD and Stan who were both grinning like freakin' idiots at Mrs. Smith's question directed at him.

"Why not nab these other yahoos? Why me?" he repeated in a mortified whisper. Bad enough that he and his friends were privy to this conversation; he didn't want the entire senior citizen kingdom to hear as well. They probably heard anyway. Beside the bodily function obsession, he'd noticed another thing about seniors. They liked to mind everybody's business.

"I already asked them. They're gonna." Obviously, Mrs. Smith had no inclination for hushing, as demonstrated by her booming voice. She'd probably forgotten to put in her hearing aid, and didn't realize how loud she was taking.

Gonna? What kind of word is gonna for a former teacher? And, son of a gun, "gonna what?"

"They are?" Sam was flabbergasted as he gazed at his two best friends in the world. Both of them nodded vigorously, barely stifling their laughter.

Well, he didn't think it was so damn funny.

"Yep. So, do you do tricks?"

"Not lately," he gasped out. Not ever, actually.

"Well, everyone on this bus earns his keep. Can't just stand around looking pretty, Mr. Hotshot Black Angel."

"It's Blue Angel, not Black Angel," he corrected her. He was beginning to get miffed with Mrs. Smith's abrasive attitude.

"Blue, black . . . whatever . . . you could be a purple angel for all I care." She glared at him. "What's your specialty, boy?"

Oh, my God! The old bat wants me to screw for money. Can my life go any further down the tube? I can't believe that JD and Stan agreed to this. And how the hell do I know what my specialty is?

Mrs. Smith had a clipboard braced against one of her forearms, and she was tapping a Scooby Doo ball point pen on it impatiently, waiting for his answer. The pen was probably one of the many donations made to the Santa Brigade effort. "Tap, tap, tap, tap, tap . . . " Mrs. Smith still waited for his answer.

"Do . . . do tricks with whom? Senior citizens? Homeless people? Isn't that sort of taking charity to the extreme?" He tried not to appear as revolted as he felt.

Mrs. Smith blinked at him rapidly, clearly confused. Then she reached over Stan and whacked him atop the head with her clipboard. "Once a moron, always a moron, Merrick. I was talking about magic tricks . . . to be performed at homeless shelters. Good Lord! What gutter have you been living in the past fourteen years?"

With that, she turned on her ample legs, knee-high stockings bunched at the ankles, and stomped away, muttering under her breath. Then, just before she reached the exit door, she tossed out, "I'll give you 'til nine a.m. tomorrow morning to decide what entertainment you'll provide, or you'll be off the bus. And don't think I can't do it."

"Way to go, Einstein," Stan said with a guffaw of laughter, clapping a hand on his shoulder so hard he probably bruised a shoulder blade . . . a hand which had, no doubt, been insured by Lloyds of London at one time when he'd been a star NFL quarterback. JD reached across the table, offering him a napkin to wipe away the coffee he'd apparently sprayed in front of him during his choking fit.

"I knew what she meant," he lied, hoping his heated face didn't give him away.

"Yeah, right!" JD and Stan hooted at the same time.

"Speaking of the Santa Brigade," Sam said, trying to change the subject, "It's as if I've fallen down the rabbit hole to an Alice in Wonderland Christmas mad house, but I've got to admit I'm really impressed with these characters and the shows they put on."

"Damn straight!" JD agreed.

"You know, part of the success of the Blue Angels is the ability to put together and break down all the equipment necessary for an air show in the most efficient manner . . . day after day, city after city, for six months. To a smaller extent, that's exactly what this troupe does. Each person has a role, not just in the entertainment, but in packing up, soliciting gifts . . . " he shrugged, " . . . everything."

"Well, you have to give Reba credit for that," JD said.

"Speaking of Reba, how's it going between you two?" Stan asked.

"It's not."

Both of his pals laughed at his woeful tone of voice.

"Even his heroic skydiving caper didn't impress her," JD told Stan. He could tell JD was having a grand ol' time, at his expense.

"It impressed the hell out of me when I heard about it," Stan said.

"Where did you hear about it?" A sense of foreboding came over Sam.

Stan waved a hand airily. "Oh, everywhere. The radio, the New York *Post*, the *Today Show*. Man, oh man, you shoulda heard the morning talk shows rave about how romantic you are."

Sam said a foul word, then confided sheepishly, "Reba called it a juvenile prank."

"Aaah, but I bet, deep down, she was all melty." JD smirked as if he'd just expounded some great wisdom.

"Melty? Melty? Is that a private eye word?"

JD wagged his eyebrows at him. "Slick, Slick, Slick, maybe I should give you lessons in charm since your legendary talents in that department have apparently worn out. In fact, some people lately have compared me to Harrison Ford . . . when he was younger."

"Are you delusional?" Sam scoffed. "What's next on your career agenda? Indiana JD?"

JD grinned and reached across the table to swat him playfully on the arm. "You're not the only one who can have movie star good looks, pretty boy." Both JD and Stan were laughing uproariously.

"Cut it out, you two. The manager is scowling at us," he grumbled. "And the Senior Santas are getting an earful."

Stan started to tap his fingertips on the Formica table top, thoughtfully, then offered, "You wanna know what I think, Slick?"

Actually, no.

"I think you need to try a different tack. It's like football, if one play doesn't work, improvise."

Hmmmm. One of the Blue Angels' mottos is, "Observe, Study, Adjust." Could that work?

"I think," JD added, "that charm works only when you're bulletproof, and, Slick, you were never bulletproof when it came to Reba."

That was really helpful.

"I don't give a rat's ass what either of you think. Unless you guys have some concrete suggestions, can the goofball opinions."

"Okay. How about this?" JD said, then made a suggestion that was so outrageous, and explicit, that Sam's mouth dropped open. He didn't look, but he could swear he heard the clicking of several dropped dentures, too.

"That could work, that could work," Stan remarked. And he was serious.

"By the way, do the Blue Angels allow you to skydive at will anywhere you want?" JD inquired. He batted his eyelashes at him as if he already knew the answer.

"Hardly."

"Yeah, I was wondering about that, too," Stan joined in. "I would think the Navy would be calling you in for a court martial, or at least some of that KP shit. Or is that only in the Army?"

"I'm in a little bit of trouble," he admitted. Actually, his superior had left three voice mail messages on his cell phone thus far, which he hadn't yet returned. "But I'll be okay. At the moment, they want me more than I want them."

JD and Stan frowned with confusion, but he didn't want to get into that career discussion just yet.

Seeing that he wasn't going to elaborate, JD said, "Back to Reba and how you can get her to talk to you. Before you proceed any farther with your charm assault . . . and don't tell me any different . . . I know you'll charm her over, eventually . . . well, I have to ask, are you thinking clearly?"

"Huh? You mean, about Reba?"

"Hell, yes, about Reba. I mean, she was a good friend to all of us when we were growing up in Snowdon. I'd hate to see her hurt by you . . . again."

"Hey, hey, hey! I was hurt, too . . . when she got married," he said defensively.

"Reba's married?" Stan was clearly shocked. "You're hitting on a married woman?"

"And no one, including George, ever bothered to tell me when she got divorced," Sam continued.

"Reba's divorced? No one even told me she got married," Stan griped. "What am I? The potted plant in this threesome? I thought we were best friends—for life."

Ignoring Stan, JD stared pointedly at Sam. "Bottom line, buddy, are you trolling for a little action here? Or something more?"

"I wish I knew. I've gotta tell you, I've been undergoing a severe case of career burnout lately. Good thing my tour with the Blues is just about over. It takes total dedication and concentration to fly those maneuvers, and I'm not sure I have it anymore. I know it sounds crazy, but suddenly I feel as if I've been running as fast as I could for the past fourteen years and only lately discovered that, in reality, I've only been running in place."

To his surprise, his two friends didn't look at him as if he'd gone off the deep end. In fact, they nodded their heads in understanding.

"You asked about Reba, JD. Well, all I can say is when George told me that Reba was the tour director of this Santa Looney Tunes Brigade and that she wasn't married, it was as if the blinders had fallen off my eyes. I felt happy and hopeful for the first time in ages." He shrugged. "What do you suppose that means?"

JD and Stan exchanged a knowing glance with each other, then turned to him. Simultaneously, they informed him, "You're in love."

Sam was going to protest, but he wasn't sure they hadn't hit the answer right on mark. The question was, What was he going to do about it?

Luckily, he was saved from having to answer that question, even to himself, by Stan. He was speaking to JD, "So, what's with you and the Amish chick?"

"Where is she anyway? I thought you were afraid she would run away," Sam added, glad to no longer be the center of conversation.

JD's face flushed a nice pink color before he murmured, "I handcuffed her to the bed back in our room."

"Holy shit!" Stan exclaimed.

"I've been meaning to give you some advice," Sam said to JD, his lips twitching with suppressed mirth. Time for JD to get a dose of his own medicine.

JD snorted with disgust.

"Really. You're screwing an Amish woman? For chrissake, JD, an Amish woman is just one notch below a nun. And handcuffs? Tsk-tsk-tsk! Even for you, that's kinda perverted." The whole time he spoke, Sam grinned, wondering if he might borrow the cuffs himself. That would be one way of getting Reba to sit still and listen to him. And after she talked to him, well, who knew what use they could be put to?

"Until tonight, Reba has been wearing that Jolly Ol' Fat Boy outfit," JD apprised Stan. Then he turned with seeming innocence to Sam. "Speaking of perversions, loverboy, where does having the hots for Santa Claus fall on the perversion scale?"

"I heard about this on the Internet," Maudeen, the Cyber Granny, piped in then. To the surprise of all three of them, her purple spiked head was peeping up over the back of JD's seat. She must be kneeling on her own bench seat, and, apparently, she'd been eavesdropping on their conversation. Surprise, surprise!

"Heard about what?" the three of them inquired at the same time. Which was a mistake . . . a big mistake.

"Sex perversions," she answered matter-of-factly. "In fact, I accidentally landed on a website yesterday dedicated to sex with dwarves. Can you imagine that?" She shook her head at them. "Nuns, Santas, Amish, dwarves, all the same fetish, I guess."

"Actually, in the Santooian Mountains, sex with the god of winter, which could be construed to be St. Nicholas, is considered a blessed event." Speaking now was Dr. Meg, expounding from her anthropologist role.

"Ah, I remember now," her sister, Dr. Maggie, said, "how icicles in the form of penises were used to decorate trees during their festivals. And they were flavored with herbs that the women sucked on to increase fertility."

"Where'd you say those mountains were?" It was Morey Goldstein speaking now, a former butcher from Bangor and the self-proclaimed stud muffin of the senior citizen community. He popped his bright red suspenders and winked jauntily at the two sisters. Morey had a collection of two hundred pairs of suspenders. Sam knew because Morey had regaled him for hours today with details about every one of them.

The twins reacted to Morey's question and his wink with soft giggles.

Now, I've seen it all!

"There's nothing perverted when two people love each other," the soft-spoken Ethel Ross remarked. She and her husband John were sitting in the next booth across the aisle, holding hands, as usual. If there were ever lifetime lovebirds, it was these two, who'd been married for fifty years. He knew because they'd regaled him for hours today with details about every one of those years.

"That's right, Samuel. Try anything you can, anything, if you really love Reba," John advised as he exchanged a look with his wife that clearly said they had personally tried it all themselves.

Oh, swell! I really need that picture in my mind. Two old people getting it on!

"What was that you were saying about landing in Alice in Wonderland's rabbit hole?" Stan asked him.

"I'm beginning to think we all landed there," JD said, "or else Bedlam."

The seniors began to exit then, waving cheerily to them as they passed by, and calling out, "Merry Christmas" to the diner staff. It wasn't surprising that the owner of the restaurant had packed up several cartons of nonperishable foodstuff for them to take to the next homeless shelter.

"They seem really nice," Stan observed when they were all gone.

"Wait 'til they start interfering in your life," Sam warned.

"Hah! They already have," JD said. "That bus must have passed by a half dozen towns with sheriffs' offices today, but would Betty Morgan stop? Nosirree. She came up with more damn excuses why she couldn't veer off her scheduled route than Lucky Charms has marshmallows. There's no question in my mind that the ladies on this bus have been conspiring to protect Callie."

"From you?" Sam asked.

"From the law."

"Oh, that's right, you already told me she's an FTA. That means failure-to-appear," he told Stan, impressed with his own ability to have remembered that bit of bounty hunter lingo.

"Why would the members of the Santa Brigade want to protect a criminal?" Stan wanted to know.

"She's not really a criminal. At least, I'm not sure she is. She's a star witness in a federal racketeering case, and she disappeared the day her court testimony was due. But I think the Santa ladies have ulterior motives for harboring Callie. She's a famous designer, and they've enlisted her to help with dressing some old Barbie dolls they received yesterday. If they don't get them dressed, they can't give them out tomorrow, or Thursday."

Stan put his face in his hands, then shook his head like a shaggy dog. "Hold the train . . . uh, bus . . . here, JD. What does the Amish woman, sheriffs and FTA have to do with each other? Better yet, what dress designer?"

"Callie is *the* Callie of Callie Brandt Originals."

"Holy Smoke, JD! She's as famous as Donna Karan or Vera Wang."

"Who the hell is Vera Wing?" Sam was addressing Stan. "You know the names of women's dress designers?"

"It's Vera Wang, you lunkhead," Stan laughed. "And who hasn't heard of Callie Brandt? She designed a bunch of the gowns for the Oscars last year."

"Well, this just takes the cake! An ex-NFL football player who's into dress designs!"

"You wanna make something of it?" Stan growled just before poking him in the ribs with an elbow. Between the overhearty shoulder whack and this jab, not to mention Mrs. Smith's head bang with a clipboard, he was going to be black and blue.

Then he turned his attention back to JD "And you have *the* Callie Brandt handcuffed to your bed? For the love of Mike, JD, you are in big, big trouble."

Instead of disagreeing, JD nodded with a self-deprecating grimace.

It was Stan's turn to play catch-up.

"How you doing, buddy?" JD stared pointedly at the cane propped against the table, near Stan's knee.

"I'm okay," Stan answered, but the lack of enthusiasm in his voice belied his assurances. "With continued therapy, this gimp leg should be near perfect. Once I get this shoulder back the way it should be, I won't suffer so much pain, either. But my football days are over, guys."

A prolonged silence hit their booth then as each contemplated Stan's prognosis.

"Dammit, I'm thirty-two years old. I probably would have had to quit in a year or two anyway as these old bones grew creaky. But I always said I'd go out in a blaze of glory, not through the blaze of a distracted driver." The bitterness in his voice was telling.

"What will you do now?" JD asked.

"Hell if I know."

"Do you need any cash?" Sam inquired. "I have a little stashed away."

Stan laughed. "Thanks for the offer, but money is the least of my problems. Truth to tell, I've made a ton this past year, but not from football. It seems I have the Midas touch in picking stocks."

"Like how Midas?" JD wanted to know.

"Like one million profit on Dilly.com, alone. And another mil on some medical stocks. Like I said, I seem to have the knack."

He and JD just gaped at their friend. Who would have guessed it, when they were raggedy orphans back in Snowdon, that one of them would turn into a regular Warren Buffet.

"And the woman with you? Dana? Is she someone special?"

"Nah!" Stan said. "I mean, she's special, all right, with those great legs of hers." He smiled to himself as if picturing those very legs. Probably in some interesting positions. "She's a friend of George's. He asked me to pick her up along the way."

When Stan was done talking, a comfortable silence prevailed.

"No matter what our problems might be at the moment," Sam said suddenly, "you have to admit, we've come a long way from Snowdon."

"Yep," his two good buddies concurred.

Sam planted his elbow in the middle of the table, a signal for the multiple-handed shake that had been a symbol for their friendship from way back. The other two put their elbows on the table, as well, and all of them clasped hands, one on top of the other. Tears of emotion rimmed all three sets of eyes.

"Friends Forever," they said.

There was something missing from this picture, though. It was supposed to be a four-handed shake, not just three. Reba had been their best friend, too.

Sam vowed then and there. He was going to get Reba back, come hell or high water . . . or Santa Brigade. As a military man, he knew how to plan assaults. He had weapons. He was Slick. If nothing else, she was now his target. Let her just try to escape his cross-hairs.

Reba didn't stand a chance.

About the Author

Sandra Hill is the bestselling author of more than thirty romantic humor novels. Whether they be historicals, contemporaries, time travels, or Christmas novellas, whether they be Vikings, Cajuns, Navy SEALs or sexy Santas, the common element in all her books is humor.

As the mother of four sons and the loooong-time wife of a stock broker, Sandra says that she had to develop a sense of humor as a survival skill in the all-male bastion she calls home. (Even her German Shepherd is a male.) And as a newspaper journalist, before turning to fiction, she managed to find a lighter side to even the darkest stories.

It's been said that love makes the world go 'round, but in Sandra's world, love with a dash of laughter, makes it spin.

CPSIA information can be obtained at www.ICGtesting.com
Printed in the USA
BVOW012018221211

278967BV00001B/58/P